MW00914972

My Knight Before Christmas

Amanda P. Jones

Pine Lake Publishing, LLC

Cover design by Melody Jeffries Design

Edited by Megan Clements

www.authoramandapjones.com

♥

To my Romance Writer's Movie Night Group
For all the kisses, throat punches, and laughter.

One

My date's sweaty palm gripped my cold and clammy one as he recounted *another* story of his pet guinea pig, Petal, whose funeral we were at. That's right. Instead of postponing our date, Felix thought I'd enjoy nothing more than attending his "*best friend's*" life celebration.

With the hand not being held captive, I tapped on my cell screen lying next to me on the picnic blanket. Forty-five minutes had passed since we arrived in Felix's backyard.

They were by far the longest minutes of my life.

He hiccupped midway through his latest retelling. "And then, right in the middle of breakfast, Petal figured out how to use the step stool in the kitchen to hop up on a chair, then a barstool, until she was on the counter eating pancakes right off the plate!"

Could small pigs really do that? Actually, any pig?

"She was just so special," he rambled on. "What am I going to do without her snout pressing up against my cheek every day?" He brought our clasped hands up to his face, nuzzling our fingers. I slowly slipped my hand out of his, reaching for the sandwich I'd yet to eat because of my hand-jailer. I attempted a one-handed approach of my sub earlier, but my tomato and lettuce fell off. Seriously, didn't he know food like this required all ten fingers to consume? Felix did not think through this date at all.

When I didn't respond, he launched into another tale of Petal. This one made tears fall by the gallons. Oh boy.

Pets were like family. I got that. My sweet poodle, Roxy, had passed away my senior year of high school. Whenever I glimpsed the picture my parents kept on our mantle, my heart pinched. Her downy fur and round eyes would never again greet me when I visited my childhood home. But we grieved in private.

After I finished the last bite of food, I interrupted Felix. "It's getting late, and I think you need some time to process everything. Will you drive me home now?"

"Oh." He startled. "Right. Yes. Let's go."

I stood, wiping my hands down my backside. "Thank you."

We drove back to my house in complete silence. Not even the radio was on. I kept my gaze trained out the window, not caring if I came across as rude. Felix hadn't asked me a single question about myself tonight.

What happened to all the good men in the world? The ones who held steady jobs, moved out of their parents' basement, kept up on personal hygiene, and didn't take their date to a funeral? Were they taken already? After another failed first date, the answer was clear and simple: yes. Yes, they were.

When Felix pulled into my driveway, I assumed he'd drop me off and go. Much to my horror, he followed me to my door. Did he want a goodnight kiss? I shuddered. Not. Happening.

I stood on my porch; the light shining on him. If he were someone I had any sort of attraction to, the glow over his red hair could be romantic. The look of pure misery on his face matched my own. *I hear you, buddy. This date was not at all what I agreed to either.*

"Well," I said, puffing my cheeks out. "I hope you drive home safe, Felix." I held out a hand for him to shake.

"Do you want to go out again sometime?" he hesitantly asked.

Uhhh, pretty sure he'd been with me the last hour and not a single moment sparked any *let's do this again* feelings. If anything, it cemented the fact that my roommates, Anna and Amy, were wrong with a capital W. The newest, hottest, dating app, that was "sure to bring me a boyfriend within a year", had failed me.

At twenty-five years old, I knew I still had time to find the man of my dreams. But Mom kept asking for grandbabies, and my roommates had ridiculously adorable boyfriends. Why was it so easy for them to find a match, but not me? What was wrong with me that always drove men away? Was I too clingy? High maintenance? Did I not show enough interest? How would I ever get my happily ever after, which included making Mom a grandma? If I couldn't find one now as a perky woman in her mid-twenties, what hope was there the older I got?

As my one-year Kismet anniversary approached, I'd yet to find a single man to become serious with, let alone go out with, twice. Well, except for Liam, but I refused to think about him or the six dates we went on.

All in all, online dating was a big fat waste of time—and not for lack of effort on my part. I went out almost every weekend and, occasionally, on weeknights too. Granted, my schedule was wonky due to working at a bakery, but I'd found a way to squeeze in both: caffeine.

For Amy and Anna? They met their boyfriends within three months. Not poor old me, Avery Thatcher. (Yes, Amy, Anna, and I were called Triple A *all* the time. No, we could not provide any assistance, roadside or otherwise.) So why couldn't I find a significant other? Most people said I was cute. I had classic features: wavy brown hair, hazel eyes, an average figure, and an appropriate laugh. On occasion, Aunt Flo pestered me with *slight* mood swings and a smattering of zits, but who didn't she curse?

Despite my flaws, I determined this would be the year I met someone special. My roomies agreed. I'd been down on my luck for so long, fate had to smile on me eventually.

Tonight was not that night. "Felix," I said, gentle but firm, "you should take some time for yourself and grieve. Petal will occupy your mind for a little while, and I don't want to distract you from that." Or go on another date with you.

He nodded as if I bestowed Mother Teresa's level of wisdom on him.

"Best of luck," I said quickly, opening my front door and practically slamming it behind me. I blew out a large breath and slid down the back of the door until I was on the tiled floor. My forehead rested on my knees. Why did I keep doing this to myself? When did I admit insanity?

"Date went that well, huh?" Amy asked, stopping in front of me in our entryway. I pulled my head up to meet her gaze. Even though she was in yoga pants and a t-shirt, with her blonde hair swept up in a messy bun, she was gorgeous. No wonder she found someone through the dating app so quickly. I swear my thumb had a callus from all the swiping on Kismet the past year.

"We can add it to the book," I replied. We kept a spiral notebook on top of our refrigerator where we documented our worst dates to help process what happened. There were quite a few doozies in there. Mine took up the most space.

Amy's face crumpled. "Oh sweetie, I'm sorry. Someone out there is just waiting to meet you. We need to keep looking."

My stomach dropped out as if I were on a roller coaster. At what point did I give up? It was as though I was a dinghy on rough seas. My white flag rested on my lap, and the universe cackled, while sending storm after storm, wondering why I hadn't raised my arm in defeat. "Fly," the white flag begged, "fly!"

"You'd tell me if it were me, wouldn't you?" I asked. "I mean, I'm the common denominator in of all these miserable dates. Am I too picky?"

Amy pulled me to my feet, leading me to the couch. "Sit," she commanded. I obeyed like an obedient hunting dog.

She went to the kitchen, coming back with the only tribe who hadn't let me down. Tillamook. She placed the creamiest, chocolatiest ice cream on the planet on the coffee table before handing me a spoon. Not that I needed anymore sugar, but I never said no to chocolate.

After a few bites, Amy looked at me head on—her game face intact—which meant I was about to be complimented until my ears burned or given a reprimand for my self-pity, also causing said ears to burn.

"I think you're not picky enough," she announced.

My stomach tightened. "It's not like I'll date just anyone. I have standards. You and Anna always approve the men's profiles before I agree to go out."

She nodded. "True, but remember all the horrible guys I went through before finding Lucas? I have a lot of doozies in the book too. Besides, we can't force our men on you. Remember how well that went with Jackson?"

Ah, yes, Mr. Attorney, who only spoke about his cases. They thought his profile was perfect. Too bad he never mentioned his addiction to his profession before our date. Huh. They should add that feature to the app. I could easily admit I was obsessed with chocolate, rom-coms (in any form: book, movie, real life), and yoga.

"Anyway," Amy continued as I dug around for another scoop of heaven in a carton. "I don't want you to give up. Not every man is a loser or will end up cheating on you. I know what your aunt and uncle did to each other makes it hard for you, as well as your scummy ex-boyfriends, but I promise there's someone out there who is ready to love you the way you deserve."

My chest constricted the same way I squeezed a bag when piping frosting at work. Growing up, we spent every holiday and all summer with my extended family. I didn't notice the tension until I became a teen, but our gatherings were the equivalent of either piña coladas on the beach or tip toeing over hot coals. All because of my aunt and uncle.

They cheated on one another so often throughout their marriage, no one knew why they stayed together; or what version we'd get at family parties. The happy, loving couple, or the feuding jealous rivals? It really made me worry about who I trusted because if those two could continue hurting each other like that, who was to say I wouldn't choose a man who'd do the same to me? I'd already picked wrong in high school, and then again in college. Liam hadn't helped when he ghosted me.

"I'm going to delete my profile on Kismet," I resolved.

"Guess what?" Anna burst into the house, shouting with glee. Her golden brown locks flowed freely down her back, her blue eyes sparkled.

"You went shopping?" I guessed. Anna was always dressed to impress. What was wrong with good ol' jeans and a t-shirt?

"Sadly, no." she clucked. "But Spencer got that new marketing manager job, and he's having a party Saturday night to celebrate!"

Anna adored parties like one adored puppies. Probably because she was an event coordinator and loved any opportunity to throw a shin-dig. They weren't my cup of tea.

Amy jumped up, hugging her. She was the sweetest of us three. "That's so exciting. What should we wear, and what should we bring?"

"You gals have fun," I said, digging my spoon into the melting ice cream.

Anna put her hands on her hips. "You have to come!"

I slowly shook my head. "No. I don't."

Amy chimed in. "Avery, maybe this would be a good night to have some fun without stressing about another date."

I pointed my spoon at the two of them. "And watch you two cuddled up to your boyfriends all night? No thanks."

"That will be hard to do when Spencer is inviting twenty to thirty people," Anna said.

Amy sat next to me and grabbed my hand. "Please come, Avery. We won't have as much fun without you."

Lies. They would probably have more fun without me bringing the party vibes down.

Anna sang, "It's casual attire, and he's having Big Doc's BBQ cater."

I would have gone—kicking and screaming—to the party because I loved Anna, and her boyfriend, Spencer. But if Big Doc's was catering, I would be there without a fight. It was hands down the best barbeque in Lampton.

"Fine. Count me in." I scraped my spoon against the bottom of the container. How had I eaten the rest of it already?

Amy and Anna turned to gape at me with matching shocked expressions. "Did she just—" Anna said at the same time Amy mouthed, "She said yes?"

"Ha-ha. I know this is big and I wouldn't miss it."

Anna's head tilted as she studied me. "Are you bringing someone? Is that why you're so amenable?"

Her comment stung. I supported my friends all the time, even if I fought about it first. Why would this be any different? "No. I'm done with men for a while."

"Even if Liam waltzed back in your life?" Anna challenged with a sparkle in her eye.

My heart slammed into my throat. In the extremely long months of dating via Kismet, Liam was the only one I went out with more than once. I fell fast for his giant smile and humor. The way he spoke passionately about traveling the world and basketball. How excited he got when a client loved his marketing campaign. How open he was about his feelings.

When we went ice skating on our second date, anytime our hands brushed, or we held on to the other's arm for balance, heat and tingles took over my body. It was like eating a warm brownie with ice cream and fudge on top. After our sixth date and first kiss, he said he'd call me later. I never heard from him again. He ghosted me.

"Stop it. Liam's ancient history." Ancient as in three months ago. I had thought after meeting Liam that the app really had made my dreams come true. Too bad it only lasted a month before my string of bad luck caught up to me. One good month out of twelve did not mean dating and I were on good terms. And as of tonight, any terms at all. I meant it when I told Amy I was deleting my account. For good.

Of course, my traitorous cheeks heated as I recalled the way Liam's strong arms wrapped around me. Ugh. Why did they have to bring his name up? I stood, ignoring my roommates, and went to the kitchen to dispose of the empty ice cream carton.

"You never know," Anna taunted after me.

Uh, his silence for the past three months said plenty on the matter. We were over.

After washing my hands and putting a bag of popcorn in the microwave I hollered, "Anyone up for *The Proposal*?" I might as well enjoy someone's happily ever after seeing as mine was buried six feet under.

Both girls agreed, and we spent the night curled up on our overstuffed couch, caught up in Ryan Reynolds's hypnotic brown eyes.

After the movie, while brushing my teeth, an image of Liam—who should not be allowed to appear any time my mind saw fit—flashed in my memories. I suddenly inhaled sharply. My throat spasmed as stinging toothpaste burned my mouth to smithereens. I coughed, splattering foamy bubbles everywhere.

Enough. I would attend Spencer's party with one goal in mind. Okay, two. First, eat the best barbeque in town. Second, get Liam out of my mind for good.

"Hurry up, Avery, we're going to be late," Anna called from the front door.

I tugged my leather sandal strap over my heel, while hopping on one foot, and grabbed my clutch before meeting Anna and Amy in the entryway.

"If you didn't demand I change my clothes a million times, I would have been ready an hour ago," I complained.

"Casual does not mean jeans and a t-shirt," Anna retorted.

Anna and I were so different. We were on separate planets when it came to fashion. She was Nordstrom; I was Target. Although, in her line of business, first impressions were a big deal. I was often covered in frosting and flour.

"You look great, Avery," Amy jumped in. "Let's go, so we aren't late."

"My dress does look fantastic on you," Anna agreed, roving her eyes over my body.

The navy sundress with the tan skinny belt accentuated my curves and played up my eyes. "Thank you," I said.

We climbed into Anna's car. Anna and Amy in the front, me in the back.

"How's your class doing?" I asked Amy, who taught second grade.

"I'm proud to report Dominic passed off his sight word list yesterday," she announced. "Of course, he negotiated to get a Tootsie Roll for each word he read."

I smacked her shoulder. "And you gave it to him?"

She peered over her shoulder at me. "I was out of stickers. So, yes, I did."

Anna and I chuckled. "You're a good teacher," I said. "A pushover sometimes. But the kids adore you." I assisted Amy in her classroom when she couldn't get parents to help. She was so patient with them. I wished I had more of her qualities.

She turned over her shoulder to look at me. "I have a good class this year."

Speaking of jobs reminded me the bakery I worked at would soon be chaotic. "Can you believe Meg leaves for California to film *Baking Spirits Bright* in three weeks?" I asked. My boss, Megan Frost, was competing in a Christmas baking show to get more exposure for the bakery. I'd been assigned manager duties while she was gone. I was only slightly freaking out. Not that I would tell Meg that. She panicked enough over leaving her bakery in my hands.

"I swear you were just telling us she applied for the show," Anna said. She merged onto the freeway toward her boyfriend's house.

I filmed Meg's audition almost six months ago. How had time passed so quickly? "It seriously feels like it. What if I mess something up? I'm not sure I'll remember everything Meg told me," I moaned.

Amy turned around in her seat, facing me. "You'll be great, I promise. And if you need help, we're here." She pointed between Anna and herself.

"Well," Anna grimaced. "I have two parties coming up, so my time is limited. But absolutely. If you need us, we'll be there."

"You gals are the best." I placed a hand on each of their shoulders and squeezed. "So, who will be at Spencer's?"

Amy and Anna shared a wide-eyed look again. Anna met my gaze in the rearview mirror before darting back to the road.

I raised my brows and tilted my head. "What's happening?" I pointed between the two of them.

Amy shrugged.

Right. And I was a monkey's uncle. "Y'all are dropping Texas-sized hints that *something* is going on. Why won't you just say it?"

Anna responded without taking her eyes off the road. "Does it matter? *Tonight will be fun.*" Her face was the same as when she forced me to go to a haunted house during our freshmen year of college. *I don't do scary.* There was enough crazy in the world that purposely seeking out fear for the sake of entertainment was loonier than tightrope walking across the Grand Canyon.

"Excuse me for not believing you," I retorted. I almost stuck my tongue out at her, but I wouldn't bring myself down to the same level as Amy's second-graders. At least, not this time.

I played with the hem of Anna's dress, stewing over their odd behavior. Obviously, they were keeping something from me, but what? And why? From their shared looks, it wasn't a good surprise. Maybe I shouldn't have come to the party after all.

Before I knew it, we arrived at Spencer's. My stomach quivered with unease. I folded my arms and set my chin at an angle. I would stay there until they told me what was going on.

Amy opened my door, pulling me out. "Come on. Barbeque is waiting."

Drat. I could already taste the ribs falling off the bone between my teeth. I smoothed the skirt of my dress, then followed my friends.

Spencer's home was situated just outside of downtown Lampton. The leaves on the tree-lined street showed off their tinges of yellow and orange as they waved in the breeze. The craftsman cottages had fall wreaths on their doors, welcoming the cooler temps with their pumpkin inspired decor. Spencer's pale-green siding, large, covered porch, and neatly trimmed bushes leading up the walkway oozed New England charm. Instead of knocking on the solid-wood door, Anna walked right in.

Music notes mingled with the rise and fall of voices. I inhaled, reveling in the tang of smoked meat. Spencer was standing in the living room, surrounded by a few guys. Anna waltzed up to him and kissed his cheek. "Hey, Babe."

"Hi," Spencer said to Anna. "You look gorgeous."

"Hey, Spencer." I gave him a quick side-hug. "Congrats on the new job. That's exciting."

"Thanks. I'm looking forward to working for Li—"

"We're going to get some food," Amy interrupted Spencer. Uh, that was a little harsh, especially for Amy.

"Good idea," Anna said. She turned wide, crazy eyes to Spencer and waved her fingers across her throat in a *cut it* motion.

Seriously, what was happening with my friends tonight? "You guys," I whined.

Amy pulled on my arm. "Let's eat. I'm starving." She led me to the kitchen, not giving me a chance to have any say on the matter. If my all-time favorite food wasn't waiting, I'd protest with a full-on tantrum.

Disposable aluminum pans from Big Doc's BBQ filled the kitchen island. My mouth watered. I almost elbowed Amy out of the way so I could go first.

"Here." She passed me a plate.

As I grabbed it from her, the sliding glass door that led to the deck opened. Two men walked in chuckling, one of whom was the last person I ever expected to see.

Liam Knight.

Three

♥

Adrenaline pumped through my veins like the Bellagio water fountains. My pulse sky-rocketed at the same time my heart screamed, *Yes! Liam's back!*

The second he made eye contact with me, the grin I dreamed about all too often appeared. His reddish-brown curly hair was shorter than the last time I saw him. His broad frame had shrunk just the slightest—not something I'd notice if I hadn't memorized his physique in our short time together.

Through the pounding in my ears, I thought I heard him say to Spencer's brother, Trent, "Excuse me. There's someone I need to catch up with."

I looked over my shoulder to see who he was referring to, but I was alone. Where had Amy disappeared to? And then it dawned on me: Liam was the reason they all acted so strange. They *knew* he'd be here. My heart beat triple time in my chest. Those lying, conniving jerks. Why would they blindside me like that?

Liam stepped toward me, and my lungs decided I no longer needed air.

"Avery," he exclaimed. "What a pleasant surprise. How do you know Spencer?"

"Anna." I managed to choke out, whether in answer to his question, or as a plea for her to save me, I couldn't be certain as my brain short-wired. "I need to go." I spun on my heel and bolted out of the kitchen, past the living room, and down the porch steps. My ankles protested the hobble I executed in my wedges. I couldn't stop, though. I had to get away from him. How could he smile at me like that? As if he hadn't dropped off the face of the planet and been captured by aliens. And his voice? How had I forgotten the smooth cadence of it?

Moments later, I heard Amy and Anna hollering my name. I didn't turn back. I kept awkwardly running at a Frankenstein sort of gait. I would text them later once I was a safe distance away.

Before too long, a stitch ached in my side. I slowed to a walk while breathing heavily. I clenched my fists. Why had my roommates kept him a secret, and why hadn't he shown any remorse for ghosting me? The least he could do was pretend to be sorry for his actions. Instead, he acted as if we split amicably and I would be delighted to see him.

Amy and Anna saw how I had moped around after he stopped talking to me. Why would they think I ever wanted to see him again? I gained seven pounds in three weeks from trying to seek comfort from any and all forms of sugar. All it left me was a sore heart and tight pants.

My phone buzzed in my pocket—another reason I loved Anna's dress. I pulled my cell out. Amy's name flashed across the screen. I silenced the call and kept walking. I had no clue where I was going, but I'd hitchhike before going back to Spencer's.

A few minutes later, Anna's silver Prius pulled alongside me. Amy, in the driver's seat, rolled the window down. "I'm sorry. We should have warned you."

I lifted my chin, turning my head away. I know I behaved like a child. My heart hurt too much to care at the moment.

"Avery, please," Amy said. "Get in the car."

"I'm not going back there."

"I'll drive you home."

I stopped, looking at her straight on. "No thanks. I don't ride with meanie heads." Wow, I was really hitting that childish behavior right on the head. I started hobble-walking again.

"You'll miss out on Big Doc's," she so helpfully pointed out.

"I think I'll survive." I wouldn't. As upset as I was about the whole Liam thing, my stomach also decided to protest the missed opportunity by not letting up with the pain in my side. "I'll call an Uber," I said.

She frowned. "This is ridiculous. Please, get in the car?"

I stopped again with my hands fisted at my sides. "No, what's ridiculous is you and Anna thinking it was a good idea to blind side me like that." I threw an arm in the direction of Spencer's house. "Not cool, Amy."

Her head hung. "I know." Her tone was so sad. So dejected.

"Why?" I asked.

"I'll explain on the way home."

I held up a finger. "Only if we stop for takeout."

She smiled while rolling her eyes. "Get in."

Walking home would take forever and I really didn't love the idea of wasting money on an Uber. Besides, side ache or not, I would have barbeque tonight, and she would get me there. I relented and got in.

I clicked my seat belt in place while she turned the car around. There was one question that kept nagging at me. "How do Liam and Spencer even know one another?"

"Liam's the one who interviewed Spencer for his new job."

"How did Spencer know he was my Liam?" My heart gave an erratic thump. He wasn't *My Liam*. I wanted him to be. Hadn't he felt the same electric current I had during our dates, which only intensified when we kissed? Obviously not. Maybe the spark I felt was really his body sending out a deterrent. One I severely misread.

"I guess Liam and Spencer hit it off," she said. "They went to lunch after his interview. Anna was able to piece it all together when Spencer told her about Liam."

"And Anna talked to you about it behind my back?"

She turned her puppy dog eyes on me. "We were trying to determine if you would come if you knew he was there. We reasoned you wouldn't, so we kept it a secret. And, I thought since you've had such bad luck since Liam, that this was the universe's way of getting you two together again. I'm sorry. We should have told you and let you decide what to do."

"If we were meant to be, Liam wouldn't have ghosted me in the first place."

"Maybe it's time to hear him out," Amy said softly.

Or maybe not.

She pulled into Big Doc's parking lot. We went inside to place our order. We didn't speak while we waited, my thoughts circling back to Liam.

How hard was it to send a text to someone? Breaking up that way was one of the worst possible options to go about it, but surely it was better than radio silence. What irked me the most was how much I still missed him. Seeing him tonight only confirmed that I hadn't gotten over him as well as I thought.

When our food was ready, Amy and I went home and ate in continued silence. My stomach felt better. However, the rest of me was heavy. I couldn't get a full breath in. Curse Liam and his gorgeous face.

Four

♥

I slept terribly last night. Too many emotions swirled inside me. It was like I was on a teacup ride at an amusement park. I held my pounding head in the palm of hand, my elbow resting on the kitchen counter where I sat on a stool.

"How are you holding up this morning?" Anna asked me as she came into the kitchen. "I got in so late. You and Amy were already asleep."

"Like you care."

Anna threw her hands up in the air. "I made a mistake. I texted you last night about how sorry I was. How long are you going to hold it against me?"

I shook my head. "I'm not happy with you, but more than anything, I'm sad. How is it after everything I still want him?" My heart throbbed along with my head.

Anna reached over and squeezed my shoulder. She wasn't big into affection like Amy and I were. That squeeze was equivalent to a bear hug in her book. "It's rare to connect to someone so quick. It isn't easy to get over that, especially with the way he left." She pressed her lips into a line and scratched her eyebrow.

I pointed at her. "You always make that face when you know something."

She busied herself by getting a pan on the stove and eggs out of the fridge. Finally, after she'd cracked her eggs, she'd said, "He told me his side of the story. I think you should hear him out."

His side of the story? What was there to tell? He got a kiss from me, and then vanished. Seems to me to speak for itself. I cupped a hand around my ear. "What's that? A pounding on the door? Oh, nope. It's silence. You're right, Liam is *very* eager to talk to me."

"He asked for your number at the party."

My spoon clattered against my cereal bowl. "He has my number."

"Actually," she drawled, "he got a new phone and lost most of his contacts. You being one of them."

Excuses. He could have messaged me through Kismet. He also knew my email address as he had to forward my ticket for our third date to the art museum, not to mention where I lived and worked. He was weaving a tale to get Anna on his side.

"Doesn't matter. I don't want to talk to him," I said.

"Please, Avery?"

My muscles tensed. "Why are you taking his side? Besides, what good would it do?"

She pointed a spatula at me. "I'm not taking his side. Maybe after you speak with him, you'll both see how great you are together."

I cocked a brow, tilting my head. "You think I want him back?" I scoffed.

"I do."

I leaned over the counter and smacked her arm. I did not want Liam in my life. "I don't."

She glared at me. "Fine. Do it for closure then."

"I have a better idea. Why don't *you* just tell me?"

She plated her eggs, going out on the balcony to eat her breakfast. Without me. She kicked the door closed on her way outside.

"Is that a 'no'?" I hollered after her.

Didn't we have a roommate code that insisted if you knew vital information, you had to share it? I shook a fist at her, then rinsed my cereal bowl, putting in the dishwasher. If Liam really wanted to speak with me, he could find me.

Five

♥

O ver the next six days, I boxed up all thoughts of Liam with two rolls of mental duct tape, and then shoved the gray blob so far back into my mind it would take a psychologist of Navy Seal expertise to track it down.

With my lunch tote and purse competing for a space on my shoulder, I made my way to the parking lot of Frostings, the bakery I worked at. As I neared my car, a tall figure leaned against it. My steps faltered, my tongue plastered to the roof of my mouth.

Why did Liam have to look so good? His straight nose, narrow jaw, and full lips made my heart reach its maximum beats per minute. Not something it was used to.

"Hi," Liam said tentatively, pushing himself off the car.

"What are you doing here?"

He shoved his hands in his front pockets. "Anna said you didn't want me to have your number. I didn't know how else to get a hold of you."

So now he was concerned about getting in touch? "And stalking me at work was the best option you could come up with?"

His head hung. "I'm sorry. For now. And before." He reached out as if to touch me then dropped his arm.

Smart move, buddy. I didn't want his hands anywhere on me. I was too afraid of the way my body would react. Memories of butterflies swooping in my stomach and heat sparking up my arm whenever he'd touched me flooded my nervous system. I'd lose all sense of control if he came too close.

"Thanks for apologizing." No way would I forgive him so easily, especially with such a weak *sorry*. I unlocked my car, dropping the bags into the front passenger seat. "I have an appointment to get to, so. . ." I walked around to the driver's side.

Liam's arm blocked me from opening the door. "Will you please let me explain what happened?"

I clenched my fists. "Go ahead."

"Not here." He tilted his head at a customer who had parked two stalls away and was exiting their vehicle.

"I'm not going anywhere with you."

His eyes turned dark. From annoyance? Pain? Frustration? All three? "You're not going to make this easy, are you?" he muttered.

"Ha," I scoffed. "You mean how you took the easy way out breaking up with me? You could have at least sent me a text." I stared at the ground as heat seared my cheeks. We never defined what we were. Never said we were an official couple. I couldn't believe I just told him I thought we were. Still, after six dates, he should have communicated *somehow* that he was done dating me.

"You're right." He kicked at a pebble in the parking lot. "And if my phone wasn't stolen, I would have explained why I had to leave town for a while. I never meant to hurt you."

Someone *took* his phone? Did they see the dozens of texts and calls I'd sent? At first, when Liam had stopped responding, I thought he was just busy. Then I worried he'd been in an accident or hospitalized. It didn't dawn on me until a week after he'd dropped me off after our last date that he was purposely avoiding me.

"I'm sorry someone took your phone. But why didn't you message or email me?"

He met my gaze. "That's what I'd like to explain to you."

I closed my eyes, inhaling deeply. He'd hurt me. Would listening to what he had to say change any of it? Probably not. At least, as Anna said, I could gain closure. Maybe then the anger and devastation would leave me be. Maybe then, when I met a nice guy, I would feel something besides numbness. Maybe then his image would stop pestering me.

"Fine. Meet me at Oaks Park by the riverwalk in half an hour." I didn't give him a chance to respond. My nerves were weakening my limbs. If I didn't get out of there, I'd surely do something embarrassing, like crumble to the ground, or punch him. The chances were fifty-fifty. My chest puffed and collapsed every ten seconds as I practiced yoga breathing. What happened that prevented his hands from opening his email and sending me a quick explanation? After dropping off my bags at home and using the restroom, where I touched up my hair and make-up (just because I was mad didn't mean I wanted to look gross), I drove to the park in silence. Even music grated my ears which wasn't normal for me.

Liam was already there, sitting on the hood of his SUV. Memories of his strong arms wrapped around my torso overwhelmed me to the point where I could almost feel his hug again. This was exactly what I was afraid of. Just his presence sent my senses into overdrive. I climbed out of my car, meeting him on shaky legs.

He hopped off his car, jerking his head toward the paved path that followed along Whittler River. I matched his casual pace, keeping a good five feet between us. As impatient as I was to hear his grand ole explanation, I bit my tongue.

Birds chirped from the branches of the oak and willow trees towering above us. The slightest breeze tickled my cheeks.

A few minutes into our stroll, he finally started speaking. "First and foremost, I want you to know I really like you. I know what I did, or rather didn't do, hurt you. For that, I really am sorry."

I side-eyed him. That apology sounded a lot more remorseful. The wall of anger I'd built cracked with a hairline fissure.

He continued. "The morning after our last date, my mom called. My Grams had a heart attack and was in the hospital."

A pit settled in my belly. Liam had told me a little about his grandma on one of our dates. He practically lived at her house in high school since he didn't get along too well with his dad.

"I booked the next flight out." His voice trembled. "By the time I got to the hospital, I only got to tell her I loved her before she passed."

I was so mad at him for ignoring me, all the while he was dealing with a devastating loss. "Liam, I am so sorry." I dared a full glance at him. His eyes were glistening.

He cleared his throat. "Thank you. Much to my, and my family's dismay, we learned I was her executor, except she didn't leave things very clear. The following three months I struggled to balance working remotely while cleaning out her house, making sure everyone got what Grams said they should, mediating disputes over what wasn't listed in the will, *and* getting her house ready to sell."

Tears pricked my eyes. I stepped closer to him, as if me being half a foot away rather than five would magically make him better. No wonder he hadn't talked to me. Did he even get time to eat while he was in Minnesota, dealing with his grandma's property? Had he even had time to grieve? Who was there to comfort him?

"I can't even imagine how difficult that was," I said. But why didn't he call me to help him through it?

"My aunt and uncle are no longer speaking to one another." He rubbed at his neck. "Half my cousins hate me now. All in all, it was a great visit home," he said bitterly.

I halted our slow steps and squeezed his shoulder. "I'm sorry you had to go through that. I wished you would have called me, even just as a listening ear." I would've flown up there to help him, if he'd only reached out to me.

His hand covered mine that rested on this shoulder. "I should have taken two minutes to message you. I regret my decision. *Every day* I regret it. I felt overwhelmed and afraid I'd scare you off with my family drama. I thought I could handle it on my own. Something I do too often, according to my sister. Before we met, I worked eighty hours a week. Meeting you forced me to reevaluate my life. I can't tell you how much you helped me—for the better. I'm sorry I didn't call you."

Oh, Liam. I would've stayed by your side through it all. "What exactly happened to your phone?"

"I lost it at the airport in St. Paul. I guess I was too flustered exiting the plane. Anyway, I called the airline hoping someone turned it in, with no luck."

"The universe was certainly against you."

"It hasn't been an easy three months, that's for sure."

"How are you doing now?" I searched his face. Where his eyes were once brilliant, they lacked the sparkle that used to be there. A wrinkle remained between his brows, as if he'd spent too much time frowning, which he probably had.

"Most days I can get through work. After that. . ." He shrugged, looking off in the distance at the river bend.

His grief was palpable. My entire being was heavy from the emotional dump truck he'd laid at my feet. I may not be able to take away his heartache and despair, but I could at least offer a bit of support. "If you ever need to talk about it, I'm here." Out of everything he could have told me, I never guessed it was this. I couldn't trust that when the next major storm entered his life, he wouldn't act in the exact same way. Because of that, I wouldn't allow him back in my life. But I also wouldn't abandon a soul in need either.

"Thank you," he said.

"Thank *you* for telling me."

He pushed a hand through his hair. "When I got home, the first thing I wanted was to call you. It's just. . . it's been hard dealing with my family and I knew too much time had passed, so I didn't. I figured you hated me, anyway. When I saw you at Spencer's, I thought it was fate bringing us back together. Instead, you took one look at me and ran. I know we can't pick up where we left off, but can we try again, Avery?"

The crack Liam left in my heart deepened. As painful as it was to admit it, I had to stick to my decision to protect my heart. "I don't think so."

If he'd asked me to marry him right after our first kiss, I'd have quickly agreed to spending my future with him, just like a cheesy romance movie. But this was real life, not some made up script. I couldn't just get over the hurt I carried for so long with a snap of my fingers. I couldn't forget the way my heart yearned for him or the month I'd spent binging sugar and going through numerous boxes of tissues while I dreamed he'd reach out to me.

"Just one date?" he asked. "If you still feel the same way, I'll leave you alone."

"I...I..." I pushed past him, running like a coward. Again. I couldn't look him in the face and tell him no, because if I did, I'd get sucked right back into his silky chocolate eyes and cave like the addict I was. When had I become a deserter instead of facing my problems?

Unlike last time, Liam chased me. "Avery, stop," he yelled.

I urged my legs to pump faster. My heart and breath were choppy. It was useless against Liam, his long legs easily caught up to me. He tugged my arm, stopping me.

Our chests heaved in unison as we caught our breath. I hunched over, resting my hands on my knees.

"Stop running from me," he huffed out.

"I'm too scared not to." My words came out breathy and stilted—partly from running, but mostly from the emotions stuck in my throat. "I don't want to be like my aunt and uncle. They continuously hurt one another and I refuse to let that be me." By allowing Liam back in my life, I repeated the same pattern I watched my entire life. I loved myself too much to be treated that way.

"I'm sorry." He shoved both hands in his hair, fisting his fingers. "I wish I'd handled it better. I wish my family wasn't so broken. I wish I'd leaned on you. Most of all, I wish you would give me another chance. Will you *please* forgive me?"

I too wished he'd done things differently. Regardless, I couldn't stay mad at him. Not when he already had too big of a burden with his family. In his place, I might have behaved the same. Withholding forgiveness would only hurt me more than it already had. "Yes," I whispered. "I forgive you."

He pulled me into him. When both of his arms came around my back, my chest melted like gooey caramel. The rest of me said, *I've missed this.* I relaxed into his embrace, allowing the moment of stillness to set my heart and mind at peace in offering him forgiveness. But nothing more.

"I promise to never do anything like that again." He pulled back to look me in the eyes. "You've been the best part of the last year for me."

I waited for the panic to set in; for the need to drown my feelings in sugar. It never came. Forgiving Liam was easy. The hard part was risking my heart again—something I wasn't willing to do. "You were the best part for me as well. But I can't dive back in." I learned some lessons from this fiasco. Ones I didn't intend to repeat.

He took my chin between his fingers, tilting my face toward his. "I'll wait for as long as you need." He placed a light kiss on my cheek then stepped away. "That doesn't mean ignoring you either. From now on, prepare to be bombarded with communication from me."

My skin tingled as if pop rocks exploded where he kissed me. A cool breeze contrasted the warmth Liam offered me, inside and out. I allowed myself to dream for the slightest moment what our future would be. Sundays watching basketball and football games while cuddling on the couch. Strolls along the beach. Nights cooking dinner together. I wound every thought like thread on a spool then threw it in the trash.

It didn't matter what Liam and I could be. I couldn't trust him to not shut me out again.

Six

As promised, Liam contacted me every day. I was in the kitchen at Frostings piping custard into eclair shells when my phone buzzed. Peeling my gloves off, I pulled my cell out of my pants pocket.

Liam: Listened to Love Sick by Maroon 5 on the way to work today. It made me think of you.

Of course I had to look up the lyrics. I was part flattered, part annoyed. Even if Liam felt that way about me, I couldn't trust him to not hurt me again. I shoved my phone back in my jeans pocket without responding. The next day, he texted again.

Liam: Mornin' beautiful. Sleep well? I've been keeping a list of everything I've missed the last few months. Here goes:

1. The beach
2. Avery's laugh
3. Fresh seafood
4. Avery's smile
5. My bed
6. Avery's silky hair
7. Watching whatever I want on TV without my sister's interference
8. Avery wrapped in my arms
9. Basketball
10. Avery's humor
11. Avery's open heart
12. Home-cooked meals
13. Conversations & my old text thread with Avery

14. Running along the boardwalk

15. Avery

I missed a lot about Liam too. His delicious brown eyes. The curls in his hair. How safe I felt cuddled up to him. His cologne. The way he could make me laugh. Our conversations about everything and nothing and never tiring of him. I responded to his text, but only about his question. I wasn't sure what to do about the rest yet. **Me:** Sadly, no. I've been going to work at three a.m. so Meg can give me the rundown. I'm tired. *GIF of someone slumping over at a desk*

Liam: Need a foot massage or some caffeine? I can stop by tonight.

Me: I appreciate the offer, but no. Anna and Amy are taking care of me.

Liam: I'll take care of you.

I held my phone to my chest and sighed. Once upon a time, being around Liam made me happy. But I couldn't let him in again. When he called me later that night, hearing his voice was like slipping on my favorite pair of sweats. Comfy. Warm. Soft. Maybe we could be friends? We talked about the upcoming Celtics season, Liam's work, more of what my responsibilities would be when Meg was gone, and our separate plans for Halloween. When I couldn't stop yawning, he said, "Night, Gorgeous. I'll talk to you tomorrow."

I fell asleep and dreamt about Liam. It was super annoying when my alarm interrupted him kissing me just below my ear. Admittedly, I was a little grouchy the rest of the day. In the middle of my lunch break the following day he asked: **Liam:** Sunflowers or daisies? You remind me of sunflowers in the way you light up a room.

Ugh. Why did he have to be so sweet? **Me:** I like both.

When I got home that night, a bouquet waited for me on my porch. I smiled like a goofball as I carried the flowers to the kitchen table. I plucked the card out of the arrangement. The note said, "Thinking of you. Yours, Liam."

He wasn't mine, although I appreciated the effort he was putting into waiting for me. The problem was, he could be waiting forever. As heart-melting as each gesture was, I couldn't move forward. Around the time I staggered into my house Thursday after work—no doubt resembling a wild-haired Princess Anna on coronation morning—my phone buzzed.

Liam: A co-worker brought in snickerdoodles today. Yours are way better.

I snorted. **Me:** I hope you didn't tell her that.

Liam: Of course not. But I thought it the entire time I was chewing.

I rolled my eyes. **Me:** You still ate the entire cookie, didn't you?

Liam: *GIF of a man saying "maybe?"*

I laughed out loud. I loved dessert as much as the next person. Even if that cookie wasn't as good as mine, I'd eat it, too.

Me: It's okay. You are allowed to eat dessert any time you want. From anywhere you want.

My phone pinged rapidly, three times in a row.

Liam: What if I only want you?

Liam: Yours. I meant yours.

Liam: Nope. I stand by both statements.

What was I going to do with this man? He was warming me up degree by degree and my heart was turning into a melted popsicle. **Me:** I still need more time.

He responded right away. **Liam:** I'm in no rush. Have you watched any good movies lately?

I went to the couch, settling into my favorite spot on the right side, my feet tucked under me. **Me:** Not any that you'd like.

Liam: Let me guess, they're all romance movies?

I scoffed as I typed. **Me:** What's wrong with romance movies?

Liam: Nothing. I'll even watch one with you.

I rolled my eyes again. Liam preferred action flicks. He'd be miserable suffering through one of my choices. **Me:** You're just saying that to spend time with me.

Liam: And. . .?

Me: I'm not ready for that.

Liam: Okay.

I appreciated him respecting my boundaries and not pushing. Yes, he extended an invitation or casually tried to see me, but every time I said no, he accepted my answer. Keeping him out of my life would be a whole lot easier if he were a monster.

Twenty-five minutes later, my doorbell chimed. Anna and Amy were out tonight, and I wasn't expecting anyone. I wrapped my cardigan tighter around my bra-free chest and opened my door so only my head peered around it. On my porch sat a plastic bag with the scent of sweet-and tangy-smoked meat radiating off it.

I picked up the package, bringing it to the kitchen table. When I opened the Styrofoam container, my favorite rib and chicken combo plate from Big Docs rested inside.

I texted Liam. **Me:** Did you have Big Docs delivered to my house?

Liam: *GIF of judge saying "guilty"* I knew you were tired and wouldn't want to cook.

Building emotion stung my nose and burned my eyes. I rubbed a hand over my face forcing the tears inside before texting him back. **Me:** That was very kind of you. Thank you.

I allowed myself to imagine what it would be like to have Liam join me while I ate. We'd sit side by side, our legs touching from hip to knee. I'd hold my fork up to Liam, offering to feed him. Our eyes would lock. My heart would race in anticipation. I'd accidentally get barbeque sauce on his lips, which I'd generously kiss off his mouth. Our food would grow cold as our kiss extended.

My stomach clenched like someone had ripped my insides out. Nope. No good would come of such fantasies. I took my plate to the couch and turned on *North & South*. Right after I snuggled into my cozy blankets for the night, my phone pinged.

Liam: Did you see the sunset? It reminded me of the time we watched one together. The light had hit your hair just right that night, making it look like gold weaved through it.

How had he noticed such a small detail? I remember that night like it happened yesterday. On our fourth date, we went to a sushi-making class. Liam had worn a fitted black tee paired with jeans that hugged his backside perfectly. The chef had to repeat his instructions multiple times because I couldn't stop staring at the gorgeous man who kept purposely brushing his fingers against mine while we made dinner.

My entire body had been on fire with Liam being so close—flirting, smiling, touching. After we'd ate, Liam had driven us to an overlook where we climbed onto the hood of his SUV and watched the sun lower in the sky. His brown eyes had been rich, deep, and entirely hypnotic. He took a piece of my heart that night, and we hadn't even kissed yet.

Me: Unfortunately, I missed it.

Liam: We'll have to catch one together another time.

I had a confused head and wobbly heart. I wanted to give Liam another chance, but my head warned me of the dangers of trusting him again.

Seven

♥

L iam: Working with a perfumery. They brought in samples of the products we'd be creating a campaign for. Not a single one smelled as good as you.

Me: It *is* hard to beat the smell of baked sugar and bread.

Liam: You have NO idea.

Another few days of texts came and went before I finally agreed to a date. I held out as long as possible, but from the moment I met him, my soul connected with his. And despite our three-month hiatus, I had never stopped liking him. No one had measured up since we dated. I quit fighting the battle and gave in. It did not mean I agreed to be exclusive with him or even considered anything past tonight, but I was willing to see where one evening took us.

"Are you sure I can pull off this outfit?" I asked Anna for the eighteenth time while I twirled in the full-length mirror. "I don't look like a professor or something?"

"Good gracious woman, you are killing me," she complained. "Yes! You look amazing. Liam won't be able to keep his eyes off you."

I asked Anna to help me get ready for my second first date with Liam. Hummingbirds had nested in my belly since he said he'd pick me up today at four. He refused to tell me what we were doing. His only instructions were to dress warmly. According to Anna, my dark jeans and striped sweater were too casual. Even if I wore a cocktail dress, she would find a fault. I switched my top out for a blouse paired with a black blazer.

I may have tackled her, asking for details of where we were going since Liam told Spencer and Spencer told Anna. But that woman was harder to crack than the CIA.

"I'm nervous," I admitted.

After our first date, we had texted all the time. Random tidbits about ourselves, memes we thought were funny, memories from our childhood. I knew his favorite song, book, movie, color, food, sport, vacation, and more. What would we talk about on our date? How did we pretend the last three months hadn't happened while maintaining the newness of dating again?

"Look at me," Anna directed. I met her determined, blue-eyed gaze. "Just like you, Liam never stopped liking you. Stop letting this," she tapped my temple, "overrule this." She touched my heart. "I know tonight might be weird at first, but try to let go of the negative and focus on the positive. Liam is not your aunt and uncle or your stupid exes. Remember that, okay?"

Right, because that was ever so easy.

"You're doing it already," she warned. "Do you remember after your second date how you made me and Amy stay up until three in the morning listening to you drone on and on about how much you and Liam had in common?"

I threw my hands up in the air. "We had an uncanny amount."

"Correction." She bopped my nose. "You still do."

I huffed out a breath. "I don't like when you're right. That's my job."

She laughed. "Not this time."

The doorbell rang, interrupting Anna's pep talk. Crazy how much I needed to hear her reassurance.

Amy's head peeked into my bedroom doorway. "Liam's here." She wiggled her brows. "He's looking pret-ty fine."

My heart galloped in my chest at the same time butterflies flitted around in my core. Focus on the positive. Liam was back. *My Liam.* The one I dreamed about six out of seven nights a week.

"Excuse me?" I glared at Amy. "Keep your eyeballs to yourself, otherwise, I'll tell Lucas you're checking out other men," I threatened.

She waved off my warning, knowing I'd never do such a thing. Lucas would never believe it, either. They were #couplegoals. At first, when Amy and Lucas, and Anna and Spencer started dating, I wanted to hear about every minute of their dates. I swooned with each of them when they rehashed (in a tad too much detail) their first kisses.

Once Liam ghosted me, I threw up a little in my mouth when they snuggled on our couch or kissed in front of me. The worst was the way they'd look at their significant others with such love in their eyes, like the world only involved around them. How could they give themselves over so completely when at any given moment, Spencer or Lucas could change their minds about Anna and Amy? Admittedly, I wasn't the nicest of friends. As such, Spencer and Lucas didn't come to our house as often anymore.

Anna and Amy did it out of consideration for me, but it was way past time for me to rectify that. Regardless of my love life, they deserved all the happiness in the world. Maybe if Liam and I worked out, the six of us could become close like in the show *Friends*.

"Don't keep Liam waiting." Anna shooed me out the door.

Holding one hand to my fluttery stomach, I made my way down the hall to the front door where Liam stood. My cheeks warmed as I took in how drop-dead gorgeous he was. Amy was right, he looked *fiine*.

I openly stared at his curly brown hair that was shorter on the sides and longer on top. He'd shaved his beard, making his strong facial features pop even more. His broad shoulders filled out a long-sleeved baby blue shirt that he'd pushed up his arms, showing off his muscular forearms.

My eyes slowly perused his body, all the way to his tan suede shoes peeking out beneath his jeans.

Anna stood next to me grinning. When I hadn't spoken in ages, still openly admiring Liam, she reached her finger up to my chin, closing my jaw. "You're drooling, Darling."

I elbowed her, which she laughed off.

"Hi," I said, in complete awe of Liam. What I really wanted to tell him was how outrageously handsome he was. But I didn't want Liam to get any ideas. The previous times I'd seen him had nothing on this version. I take that back. I was attracted to every physical thing about him. No matter what he wore, he always stole my breath. The crème de la crème? His personality. He was the complete package—except for the trust part.

"*You* are beautiful," Liam stated as a fact. Not, I look beautiful, but that he saw me, all of me as beautiful. That phrase right there was why he destroyed me so easily.

"Should we get out of here?" His eyes darted to Anna and Amy, surrounding me.

"Yes, it *is* feeling crowded."

"Have fun, you two," Anna sang, while draping an arm around Amy's shoulder. "And don't worry, we won't wait up!"

Amy's soft chuckle tickled my ear as she side-hugged me. "Have fun."

I squeezed her back before stepping toward Liam, who held the door open. I moved onto the porch with Liam following behind. He placed his hand on my lower back as we walked to his Jeep parked in the driveway. Warmth seeped into my muscles where his hand lightly rested.

Well, two things were confirmed: one, I still found Liam ridiculously attractive, and two, my body reacted to his touch in pleasant ways. This information could be the best news or the worst, depending on how tonight went.

"Sorry about my roommates," I said. "They're a little excited to see you again."

He held the passenger door open for me. His brows raised. "Are they the only ones?"

I met his gaze. "No."

He grinned, his eyes crinkling in the corners. "Good." He closed my door, going around the front of his SUV to climb into the driver's side. "Our reservation is at five-thirty, but we have a stop to make before we eat."

I clicked my seatbelt in place. "Are you finally going to tell me where we're going?"

"Nope. Tonight is a surprise."

I'd be lying if I said I hated surprises. The wait was the best part. Once the event took place, the thrill of anticipation wore off. It was just like Christmas. The month before the big day, every activity built up the excitement. Like one at a time, you added a drop of hot chocolate to a mug. Once you opened presents Christmas morning, or drank that cup, a sense of loss remained.

Yes, you still had the surprise itself to enjoy, but it wasn't the same as the exhilaration beforehand.

"Okay. I'll wait until we get there," I said, shifting in my seat so my knees were angled toward him.

He smiled. "That's one of many reasons why I like you: your patience."

"Customers help with that. Every. Single. Day."

He chuckled. "Which is why you're so good at it."

"While I appreciate the compliment, how would you know if I'm good at my job?"

He smirked. "Well, let's see." He ticked off reasons on his fingers. "We already covered you are patient. You brought me the eclairs you made before and they were the best I've ever tasted. You have a level head, which I'm sure helps you be efficient at baking and working fast. And you have a way of explaining things without being condescending like the time I didn't know the difference between a macaron and a macaroon."

Ah, yes. The great cookie mix up. Liam had picked me up at the bakery before we went on our second date. I'd offered him a freshly made macaron before we left.

"Would you like one? We just finished them an hour ago. And not to brag, but they're pretty amazing."

His smile had turned flirtatious, his brown eyes locked on mine. "Does it include you feeding it to me?"

My cheeks warmed. "Oh. Um." I was not expecting him to say that. *Way to wow him, Avery.* He'll be jumping at the chance for you to flirt back. "Yes."

He laughed, waving his palm at me. "Only teasing. I'm actually not a fan of coconut."

Not a fan of coconut? He was *so* missing out. I titled my head in confusion. "I only have raspberry, mango, pistachio, vanilla, and chocolate."

He blinked. "Coconut is literally all they're made of."

"Ohhh." I chuckled. "I see where the confusion is. So there are two types of cookies that sound similar but are different." I went behind the counter, pulling out the tray of mango macarons. "This is a French cookie. It's made with egg whites and ground almonds." I stepped to the next display case and pulled out the macaroon. "This is the coconut version you are used to that's also made with egg whites, but coconut shreds instead of fine ground almonds. The French version is petite and colorful with different flavor options. The macaroon is only coconut and bigger. Make sense?"

"So macaron and macaroon?" He pointed to each cookie as he said its name.

I nodded. "Yep."

He laughed at himself, rubbing his fingers across his forehead. "I feel foolish. How did I not know the difference?"

"Don't sweat it. A lot of people don't know."

"Thank you for educating me instead of making fun of me."

My brows had furrowed. "I'd never make fun of you, Liam."

Heat swirled around my chest, rising up my neck and into my cheeks as I recalled how Liam had looked at me with such adoration. I tucked a piece of hair behind my ear, bringing myself back to present-day Liam. "While I'm not certain all of those compliments are true, how do you do that?"

He reversed out of the driveway. "Do what?"

"See people so clearly after knowing them for such a short amount of time?"

A deep V formed between his brows. "I don't think I can do that with just anyone. At least, none of my exes would say I saw them well enough."

They were exes for a reason.

He continued, "But I also think my job helps. Finding why companies want to message their products a certain way pushes me to understand their customers. It's all a bit complicated, but the short answer is, my job and you make it easy."

"Your flattery will get you everywhere," I teased. It was a huge reason why I finally agreed to this date.

He briefly glanced over at me. "I'll remember that."

I cleared my throat. "How long have you been home from Minnesota?"

His head bobbed side to side. "Just over three weeks."

I sucked in a breath. For some reason, I assumed it had been longer. "So Spencer's party was your first week back?"

"The end of it, yeah." He nodded. "I interviewed Spencer over the phone while I was at Gram's. I arranged for us to do a second interview the first day back in the office."

"And you offered him the job by the weekend?"

He turned down a sidestreet. "Actually as he was leaving, I told him the job was his. He's got a good head on his shoulders."

When Liam said fate brought us together, he meant it. I've never believed in such nonsense before. I may reconsider. What were the odds that days after coming home, we'd see one another again?

"Spencer's a great guy," I said. "You'll have fun working together."

He turned onto the main road leading out of my subdivision. "I'm sure we will. But I don't want to talk about co-workers anymore. What were you up to while I was gone?"

Oh, you know. Getting my heart broken. Dating losers. Watching too much TV. Eating enough chocolate to feed a town. "Working. Meg's been really pushing me to take on the role of manager in her absence."

"Are you ready for the extra customers at the bakery?"

"I guess?" I put both hands out, palm side up. "I've also. . ." I gazed at the buildings we passed out my window, turning away from him. "Been dating," I whispered.

"Oh."

I whipped my head toward him at his dejected tone. One point for me for making things awkward. Why hadn't I kept my mouth shut? Trying to reassure him, I said, "Can I just say how many weirdos are out there? It's a shock you, Spencer, and Lucas were on the dating app."

His lips pulled up on one side, like he wanted to smile but didn't know if he should. "I'm trying not to take offense to that."

"You shouldn't." I bravely reached over and touched his forearm. A zing shot up my arm. "I meant it as a compliment. Also, the ten minutes we've been in the car is already the best date I've had in the past two months."

"Well." He smirked. "Maybe we should call it a night, then? End things on a high?"

I laughed. Ten minutes would not be enough. "But what about my surprise?"

"You said you didn't mind waiting."

Touché. "That's when I knew I would receive it tonight."

He tapped the steering wheel. Eventually, he sighed. "Fine. But only because everything is ready anyway."

"Wow, way to really sell it there."

He grinned. "Nothing but the best for My Avery."

My Avery? My heart flipped like a gymnast doing a back handspring. I reeled it back in before it could get too many ideas, like a future with Liam.

"How is your sister doing?" I asked to distract my tumbling heart. "I remember you saying she was close with your grandma too."

He rubbed a palm down the side of his face. "My Grams left her more money than everyone else, besides me, and my mom isn't taking it well. She feels like she deserves more even though she hasn't been involved in Gram's life the last ten years. After I left for college, it seemed their reason for talking every day vanished.

"Chloe moved in with Grams when she turned eighteen and has been there ever since. Her passing has been really hard on her."

I reached a hand over, squeezed his muscled shoulder, then dropped my hand back in my lap. "I'm so sorry. Where is Chloe moving to if you're selling the house?"

"Before I put it on the market, she decided to buy Grams' house."

My eyes bugged out of my head. "And the rest of your family is okay with that? I mean, good for her, but yikes, that seems like a tricky situation."

"My aunt and I are excited for her. We're happy the house is staying in the family. Chloe loves it there. It made the most sense."

I heard what he didn't say. I pointed at him. "But you were left to mediate the situation?"

His nod was the only answer he gave.

"I'm sure you did an excellent job of being fair on both sides."

He ran the hand not on the steering wheel up and down his thigh. "I did the best I could. I'm just sad the whole situation tore our family apart."

My immediate family was close. Imagining us fighting like that clawed at my chest. "Maybe in a few years, when emotions settle, you can reconcile?"

He offered me the saddest smile like when Eyore told his friends they'd be better off without him because his mood would bring them down. Liam looked like he didn't believe it was possible.

"Remember when you told me about that time you were in college, and your buddies took you to the barbeque joint that makes you get on the saddle when it's your birthday, and the waitress went the extra mile and gave you a kiss as well?" I asked.

He shivered. "Yeah, I do. It's hard to forget when the waitress was sixty and purred in my ear."

I playfully pushed his shoulder. "She's probably the best kiss you've had," I joked.

His eyes darted between the road and me. "Not even close."

My cheeks heated like the coils in a toaster. Because of me? Or someone else? The way he looked at me led me to believe it *was* me. My stomach twirled like a ballerina. "Anyway," I drawled, not wanting to know if Liam's best kiss came from someone else. "A little while ago, Anna and Amy, trying to get me out of a slump I'd been in, took me there. They lied about *why* we were there. Instead of saying it was my birthday, they told the staff I just found out I was pregnant."

"No," he blurted with horror.

"Yes." I slowly nodded. "They made me get up in the saddle while the waitress yelled out for everyone to join her while they sang, 'first comes love, then comes marriage, then comes the baby in the baby carriage, congratulations!'"

He leaned forward, bellowing out a laugh.

I smiled. "As if that wasn't embarrassing enough, the waitress held up my left hand looking for my 'gorgeous ring' only to see a bare finger."

"How are Amy and Anna still alive?" he asked incredulously.

I held up a finger for each reason why I refrained from suffocating them in their sleep. "Anna paid for my dinner and Amy did my laundry for two weeks. Otherwise, their bodies would be in the ocean by now."

His brows furrowed. "Why did they do it?"

I did not think this through when I chose this story. "Um. . . I. . ." I picked at the hem of my blouse. "Besides work, I hadn't left the house for a while. They were trying to cheer me up."

He cast me a worried glance. "Why hadn't you left the house?"

"How close are we to our first stop?"

He side-eyed me. "Nope, not going to work. Why hadn't you left the house?"

I knew Liam wouldn't let this go. I sighed deeply, like a child when asked to clean up after herself. I stared at my knees. "They thought the best way to move on from you was to go on another date. They wanted to prove that if I endured the most embarrassing thing they could think of, any date afterward wouldn't seem so bad."

Only they'd been wrong. So terribly wrong.

"Avery," he moaned. "I'm so sorry I put you in that situation."

I briefly touched his forearm. "I forgive you, remember? I understand how much you had on your plate. Yes, I would've waited for you if you told me what was going on, but we really weren't *together*." Forgiveness did not mean we had a future though—something I had to make sure Liam understood. "Let's just take this one moment at a time, alright?"

He turned his signal on, making a right-hand turn. "I'll always kick myself for my decisions. I was too afraid to let you in. I believed my family drama would make you run for the hills and I think subconsciously by not reaching out, it allowed me to cut ties first. As you can tell from the latest fiasco, my family has some issues which, unfortunately, I've inherited."

But he never gave me the option to choose. I worried Liam would shut me out again the next time a family issue came up. My voice came out soft. "I have forgiven you." Tears filled my eyes. "But I don't trust you. And that's why I've been reluctant to date you again."

His shoulders caved in. "If you can't trust me, does that mean we're over?"

My tears spilled over. I quickly swiped at them, not wanting Liam to see. As for us? I didn't know. I was willing to see if we could learn to trust one another again. But how long would it take? And was it worth the risk? "We need to take things one day at a time. But I also can't have you feeling like everything you do is to make up for the past. It wouldn't be fair to either of us."

He checked his side mirror before moving over a lane. "I will try to forgive myself so we can have a clean slate. And I can assure you everything I'm doing right now is because I want to. I care for you, Avery. I did then, and I do now."

So he felt our easy connection as well? Like my soul had found its missing piece that made me the best version of myself?

I chewed the inside of my cheek. "Well, I don't exactly want a clean slate. I want to remember every good part from our time before."

He reached over, slipping his fingers between mine until our palms connected, our fingers intertwined. A familiar warmth seeped into my bones, reminding me this was where I belonged.

"I agree," he said. "Otherwise, how would I know you love Tillamook and despise store brand ice cream? Or love all sorts of flowers but prefer the scent of lilac? That you'll watch basketball with me even though you like football more?"

I rolled my eyes. "I only watched one game with you." For our fifth date, Liam invited me to his place to watch the Celtics. The game was endurable because I'd nestled myself into his side. I missed that. The way my head fit perfectly on his chest while his arm draped around my shoulder, his hand resting on my hip.

I thought he'd kiss me that night. I put out every signal: licking my lips, glancing at his, indicating I hadn't kissed anyone in a while. He didn't take my bait.

I discovered Liam didn't casually date. When he met someone he liked, he went all in. For him, that meant taking things slooooowwwww. He'd told me he only had two serious ex-girlfriends. No one else ever made it past the second date.

While waiting was equivalent to mid-evil torture devices, the payoff was euphoric. A swirl of feathers fluttered around in my stomach as I recalled his lips on mine. The way he placed his hands on my ribcage, pulling me toward him. I shivered at the rush of tingles that danced through my limbs.

Which is why it hurt even more when he stopped talking to me. *We're moving on, Avery. Focus on the positive, like all the sweet things Liam has done recently.*

"That game was awesome," he said, as if he were reliving it again.

"They lost."

"I know."

"So why—"

His pointed stare told me everything. *Okay then.*

Eight

We pulled into the parking lot of the beach closest to my house. The late-September sun hung halfway toward the western horizon. The waves glistened in the distance. Very few beachgoers dotted the shoreline. A family, bundled in jackets, flew a red and yellow kite high above their heads.

I unbuckled my seat belt. "What are we doing here?" It wasn't typical beach weather.

"You'll see." He climbed out of his Jeep. "Wait a second," he said before closing his door.

Liam walked around the car, opening my door for me. I never released his hand while we were driving, only letting go once we parked. Deciding to keep the connection, I wrapped my fingers around his as we walked in comfortable silence down the wooden boardwalk. The slats creaked under our steps. A stiff breeze blew my hair to the right toward Liam. It was a good thing I hadn't worn a dress like Anna told me to, otherwise, I'd be giving everyone at the beach a peep show.

"You might want to take your boots off for this." Liam pointed to my feet.

I pulled off my black booties and socks. The cold sand tickled between my toes as we walked across the beach. Liam led us to a fallen log nestled between the waves and boardwalk. After swiping the sand away so I didn't get my pants filthy, I sat close enough to Liam that our sides touched from shoulder to knee.

Salt mixed with brine filled my nostrils. The rushing sound of waves crashing ashore spoke to my soul, lending me its strength and surety.

"This is the first time I've been to the beach since I flew home." Liam kept his volume low.

"It's one of my favorite places on earth."

He gazed at the horizon. "Growing up, we didn't have a lot of money, so it wasn't until I moved here that I saw the ocean for the first time. I fell in love instantly."

The ocean was a part of me, as much as my hazel eyes were. "I know why I love coming here, but what made you like it so much?"

He pondered my question for a moment. "The power and strength behind each wave. The depth of the water that you know hides a world we can never fully understand. That all my senses are working in tandem. That it can be fun yet dangerous, calm, yet destructive. It's all of it combined that forces me to acknowledge its magnificence while soothing me." He put an arm around my shoulders. "You make me feel those things, too."

I appreciated Liam's directness, the way he spoke openly about his feelings or shared insights into his marvelous brain and heart. I adored him all the more.

"I make you feel like the ocean?"

He shifted on the log. "Yes. You are exciting and fun yet bring me so much peace. I missed the ocean while in Minnesota. I missed *you*. I missed feeling centered and whole. And I wanted to bring you here to share one of my favorite places with you. To show you another piece of who I am.

"Throughout my childhood, my dad was so demanding. If we made the littlest mistake, he'd ream us out. I stayed out with friends as much as possible to avoid being home. It wasn't until I moved in with Grams that I felt wanted. When *we* met, it felt like I found the true meaning of home for the first time in my life. I was so afraid of messing up. It's why I took forever to kiss you. When I got back to Minnesota, and the one home where I belonged wasn't there anymore, I fell into a really dark place. I believed you would never want someone like me. I lied to myself and hurt us both in the process."

I leaned my head against his shoulder. "I'm glad you brought me here and told me all of that. Even though my hair will be a tangled mess the rest of the night." I elbowed his side, so he knew I really didn't care about my hair. "Thank you for this. For telling me. I feel like. . ."

Was it too soon to express how deep my feelings ran? Gradually, I revealed pieces of myself to Liam while we dated previously. But if I doused him with a bucket full of emotion, especially after reconciling so soon, would I scare him? I settled on something in the middle.

I inched away from him, angling my body toward his, allowing me to look into his eyes. "I know this is still new, *really* new, after everything. And while I don't believe there's only one true match for each person, when I'm with you, it's as though the sun is shining on every surface of my soul, illuminating me. I'm. . . happier."

My cheeks flamed as if the sun indeed had shined on me too long.

"I'm happier when I'm with you, too." He cupped my jaw, guiding my face to his. His chocolate eyes were pools of hot cocoa, begging me to drown in them. He placed a quick gentle kiss on my lips then pulled away before I really had a chance to process what was happening. I smiled as relief washed over me like the waves, bringing warmth straight to my heart. Maybe things would work out. Liam wasn't my aunt and uncle or my ex-boyfriends. I scooted close to him again, resting my head on his shoulder. We soaked up the view and each other for a few more minutes before Liam said we had to leave for dinner. We snapped a quick selfie then went back to the car.

The nerves clenching my stomach while I had dressed for our date dissipated. If I let my heart guide me, I'd be okay. Anna had said as much. I wasn't sure how to let go of my fears, but I wanted to try.

I looked over at Liam's profile as he drove us to where we would be eating. His straight nose, full lips, and square jaw were a sight to behold. More than that, the components that made up who he was spoke to my heart. I lived without him in my life and it was the worst experience I'd ever been through. Even with all the disastrous dates I went on, I'd do it all over again, a hundred times over, if the road always led me back to Liam.

So whether it was fate, Godly designed, or some other force, I would never take for granted the second chance Liam and I were given.

Nine

♥

He blindfolded me, and I immediately panicked. Flashbacks of the time Anna took me to a haunted house swam behind my closed eyelids. It was like the man in the white mask with the roaring chainsaw held over my head stood right in front of me.

Instead of a restaurant, Liam took me to a nature preserve. When he parked, he rushed to my door, pulling me out like my life depended on his speediness, before securing a black, silky sleep mask to my face. I slept with a night light because I hated the dark.

My heart hammered in my chest at the loss of sight. I darted my hands out in front of me, clinging to his shirt. My breath came out shaky. "Should I be worried?"

"About what?" he whispered against my ear, causing bumps to rise across my skin.

"Um, the fact that you've brought me to a secluded area, and no one knows where I am?" Teasing him hid the terror coursing through me.

He placed a hand on the small of my back, adding pressure so I'd start walking. "We won't be alone in a few minutes. Rest assured, I'm not a psycho."

His car beeped twice as Liam locked the doors. The noise startled my heightened nerves, and I jumped.

"Which is what a crazy person would say," I screeched.

He huffed out a breath. "Do you really think I'd do anything to you?"

I giggled. My fight-or-flight mode kicked in and let's just say, my brain went to loopy-town. I was NOT the person you wanted to be with in an emergency situation. "No. I'm just trying to keep from freaking out because I don't like the dark."

I knew monsters weren't creeping under my bed, regardless, I did not like being surrounded by inky blackness.

Immediately, the mask got ripped off my face. Liam's pinched eyes and worried expression stood in front of me. "I'm so sorry! I didn't know that. I wouldn't have blind folded you if I had known. I was just trying to add to the surprise. Are you okay?"

"I'm fine." Now that I could see. "But I do appreciate your cooperation in refraining from doing that again. Also, I hate haunted houses, scary movies, and other creepy entertainment."

"That's why you're staying home on Halloween?"

When Liam and I had texted about our plans for the holiday, I'd told him I usually stayed home watching movies like *Hocus Pocus* because that's the scariest I tolerated. I also liked passing out candy to the few trick-or-treaters that knocked on our door. "I like the cutesy side of it."

"Okay, that's good to know." His gaze traveled the length of my body as if he were reassuring himself I was okay. "Again, I'm sorry."

"I'll be fine in a minute."

He ran a hand through his hair, making his tamed curls frizz. He still looked hot.

"Um, but if we were going to the beach and here, why did we have to dress nice?" The sweater I chose was way more appropriate than the blouse and blazer Anna forced me into.

"Because," he elongated the word. "Of that." As we rounded the bend, a table adorned with a white tablecloth, candles, flowers, and glass flutes stood underneath a massive oak tree. The branches had outdoor lights strung from limb to limb. A round metal fire pit had flames leaping toward the sky. The scent of burning wood was so cozy and perfect for the fall evening. Soft piano notes played from a speaker. The ambience of it all took my breath away. I couldn't believe he did this for me.

A teen with black dress pants and a white button-down shirt waited for us.

"Hey Bash," Liam greeted him.

"Hi, Mr. Knight," he managed to get out with a shaky voice.

"We'll get started on our salads and sparkling cider."

"Yes, sir."

Bash moved ten yards away where a cooler and a few brown paper bags sat on a folding table.

"How do you know Bash?" I asked Liam, who helped me into my white folding chair. The oak mixed with the burning wood had me inhaling deeply. I loved that smell.

"He's my boss's son."

I placed a cloth napkin in my lap. "And how did you convince him to be our waiter? He barely looks fifteen."

Liam smiled at me as he took a seat across from me. "He's sixteen. I needed someone who could drive himself. And I'm paying him."

"Oh."

"Don't worry, he's only staying until we're done eating."

I wasn't worried about his company, merely curious. "Are you ready to play a get-to-know-you game?" I asked.

His brows raised, his chin tilted down. "Trying to take over my date?"

"Isn't this *our* date?"

"I'm the one who planned it."

I held my hands up defensively. "Didn't mean to step on any toes."

He grinned. "Thank you. Besides, don't we know a lot about each other already? I may have lost my old phone, but I still remember what we talked about in our texts."

About two weeks after he'd stopped talking to me, I went through every message we'd exchanged. I was so close to deleting them. I couldn't. An invisible force restrained my finger from pushing the little garbage can icon.

"Fine, let's recap our favorites then, shall we?" I challenged.

He smirked like he already won this competition that was all together unnecessary. "Your favorite ice cream is Tillamook Mudslide. Color, yellow. Children's book is anything by Mo Willems. On an adult level, it's anything by Katherine Center. The best football games you played were on Thanksgiving with your family. You love chocolate. I'd say it's more like addicted, but who am I to judge?" He shrugged, while holding his hands out to the side, palms facing me, in a *not me* gesture. I nodded. He'd remembered everything so far.

He continued, "Your favorite tv shows are *Gilmore Girls* and *Friends*. You loved college, except junior year because of your ex. Who, by the way," he leaned toward me, "is an idiot of epic proportions."

Again, I nodded. He was like an elephant with that impressive memory of his.

"Your favorite food depends on what you're craving, although Big Doc's wins for barbeque. You love your job but not the annoying customers."

Heat crept up my neck, spilling into my cheeks.

"Am I right so far?"

"Yes."

Bash came over, holding two plastic salad plates piled high with romaine lettuce, tomatoes, cucumbers, and croutons.

"Thank you," I said to Bash.

"You're welcome."

He left a bottle of dressing on the table then walked away allowing us to eat in semiprivacy. In between bites, Liam continued. "You're the middle child of three kids. You met your roommates in college, and you've been inseparable since. You've had four ex-boyfriends, one of which is the only one who you *think* you may have loved. Even then, you're not so sure."

I held a hand up to stop him. "Alright, I get it."

"Good."

"Now my turn." I set my fork down. "Your favorite movie is *Knives Out*. You don't really like reading, which tells me we haven't found what genre speaks to you yet. Although you did enjoy listening to *1776*, which you claim to be your favorite when pushed into an answer. You like blue but also red, so, you answer with either one or sometimes both. You studied pre-law before switching to marketing."

Bash's eyes met mine from where he waited by the cooler. His cheeks went pink before he turned on his heel in the opposite direction. Poor kiddo looked miserable watching us have our date. I took another bite of lettuce before saying more about Liam. If we scarfed our food like rabid dogs, Bash could leave.

I quickly chewed and swallowed. "You love Maroon 5, but have a secret soft spot for country music, though you refuse to admit it."

He scoffed. "I do not."

"You quietly singing along when we went ice skating said otherwise."

His eyes went wide. "I did not."

I slowly nodded my head while scrunching my nose. "You totally did."

He rubbed a hand along the back of his neck. "Fine. I admit that as a teen I liked listening to *some* country music."

I grinned. Maybe this game wasn't so bad if I got to see Liam squirm. "Sure, and I like some chocolates," I deadpanned.

He laughed. "Alright, I like country music. Okay?"

"Thank you for being grown-up enough to admit it."

His only response was to shovel another forkful of salad in his mouth.

I chuckled. "Moving on. Your favorite holiday is Christmas. You love summer and fall but could do without winter, except during December. You used to play hockey until high school when your best friend convinced you to try out for basketball. You had your first kiss when you were fifteen at a pool party."

He groaned. "Don't remind me."

"Violet wasn't a good kisser?"

He cleared his throat. "You remembered her name?"

During the darkest moments after Liam left, I wondered if my kiss drove him away. Depressed, I went into comparison mode with every woman he'd said he'd made out with before.

I stopped obsessing over it after the third date Anna and Amy forced me to go on. I knew I didn't like the guy enough for a second outing. However, when he dropped me off, he still leaned in. In a moment of pure insanity (and making sure it wasn't a *me* issue), I kissed him back.

News flash: making out with a snake would have been more pleasant. His tongue was as slimy as fish scales, and he kept his lips tight rather than loosening up when he deepened the kiss. Instead of feeling anything in the realm of pleasantness, I gagged until I pushed him away from me. I had to brush my teeth seven times before the icky feeling went away.

"Um." I took a sip of water to cool off my heated cheeks. Why had I admitted I knew her name? "Only because you mentioned her in our text messages."

He slightly shook his head, a grimace on his lips. "Right. Well, I think almost anyone would be able to top that kiss."

"That bad, huh?"

He stared at me. "Kissing my Grams on the cheek was better."

"Ewww." I held up a hand. "Don't say anything more."

He shuddered. "Are you almost ready for the main course?"

I took one last bite of my salad and nodded.

He signaled to Bash, who cleared our salads, before bringing us steak, potatoes, and asparagus on large white plates.

"How did you even keep this warm?"

"Insulated bags. Also, Bash picked it up while we were at the beach so it wouldn't get too cold."

I moaned while chewing the creamy garlic potatoes. "This is excellent. Thank you."

"Only the best for My Girl."

There he goes with the "my" again. I inhaled, causing the food in my mouth to lodge in my throat, sending me into a coughing fit. My throat spasmed. Tears gathered in my eyes. Mucus leaked out my nose. *Lovely.*

While continuing to suffer from the effects, I shielded my face with my napkin so Liam couldn't see the mess happening. Good thing I wore waterproof mascara.

Liam's movements were drowned out by my coughing, so when his hand patted my back, it startled me even more, bringing a new wave of spasming coughs.

"Can you try a sip of water?" Liam asked tenderly.

Not until I at least wiped the snot off my face. Being discreet and trying not to gross him out, all the while doing my best to keep my makeup from smearing too much, I used the napkin to dab at my cheeks and upper lip.

Satisfied I only resembled a red-blotched-faced chipmunk, I lowered the filthy napkin and gulped my ice water. Immediately, my throat found relief as the cold liquid soothed the scratchy feeling.

"Are you okay?" he asked while crouching beside me with a worried look on his face. With his body close to mine, I got lost in his gorgeous milk chocolate eyes. He had said *my Girl AND my Avery* tonight. We'd barely reconnected. Did he already see us in a serious relationship despite my telling him I wanted to take it one day at a time?

Being with him tonight *had* reminded me of how easy it was between us. How at peace I felt around him. How I was my truest self without worrying what Liam would think of me (except for when snot was on my face). I missed it. I immediately dropped eye contact, focusing on my plate. "Yes. Sorry about that." I waved a hand toward my throat.

Liam went back to his side of the table. "When I first started college, a buddy of mine became an EMT. At the time, I thought it would be a great way to meet women while helping people. Then he told me about a car accident where the driver didn't make it. That's when I decided to do pre-law instead. Every now and then, I wished I'd learned those skills."

"You can't do much for someone who is having a cough attack. Regardless, I'm glad I'm fine if you're useless in medical situations," I teased, trying to ignore what I really wanted to talk about—*My Girl.*

"Me too. How's your family been?"

I deserted my potatoes, opting for a bite of perfectly grilled steak. After swallowing, I said, "Same old, same old. My parents are about to retire. My mom is ecstatic but she worries my dad will get bored and bug her to death."

I'd chuckled when she told me he might end up in a noose. Only mom could get away with threatening dad, since she couldn't even kill a spider. She made dad capture any that came into their house and release it outside.

I cut a bite-sized piece of steak on my plate. "And my older sister loves owning her own florist shop. My brother just started his MBA program at Boston College. We see each other on holidays and random weekends throughout the year, but now that we're all adults, it's harder."

"I'm thirteen hundred miles away from mine. I get it."

I chewed my food, then asked. "Do you miss being home?"

"When I first moved here, I did. Making friends, loving my job, and meeting you helped."

My heart turned to goo like the melted parmesan cheese on my asparagus. "And now?"

He took his time eating the bite of potatoes he forked into his mouth. "Considering how messy things are, I don't miss home at the moment. I also have this pretty awesome person who occupies a lot of my time."

A soft smile grew on my lips. "Sounds annoying," I teased.

"It's not."

We finished our meal, leaving Bash to clean up.

"Are you ready for dessert?" Liam asked, holding a hand out to help me up from my chair.

I put a hand on my bulging stomach and groaned. "I'm not sure I can fit anything else in. Dinner was too delicious."

He turned a sad, pouty face on me. "That's too bad because I brought stuff to make s'mores. The fire has died down enough. It's the perfect condition for a toasted mallow."

I slapped my hand in his. "Fine. You convinced me."

He chuckled, pulling me up with so much force that I slammed into him. He immediately wrapped his arms around me. He mumbled against my hair. "That's better."

I agreed. Wrapped in his arms, I found my safe place in the world. After a few minutes, Liam let me go to get our chairs situated by the fire.

"How many do you want?" he asked, holding a paper plate filled with one graham cracker.

"One will be plenty."

He raised a brow. "Are you sure?"

I pushed his shoulder. "Yes, Liam. I'm sure."

He passed me the plate with all my ingredients separated out. I set it on my chair before grabbing one of the roasting sticks leaning against the round metal pit, putting my marshmallow on the end. I circled the fire, finding the glowing embers that would turn my white cloud of sugar to the perfect shade of gold.

Liam joined me a moment later. "These were my favorite growing up."

"Did you go camping with your family a lot?" I rotated my stick to get the side of my treat toasted.

"Yeah. It's one of the few times in my life that I have a happy memory with my dad. What about you? Do you like to camp?"

"I've only been a handful of times. My mom hates bugs, so we didn't go often. I remember liking it, though."

"What about hiking?"

"What about it?"

He pinched my side.

I squealed and jerked away from his fingers. "I literally have a flaming weapon in my hand. Watch it."

"You'd really hurt me?"

I shrugged. "Possibly."

"I will keep my hands to myself then. But will you answer the question?"

"Hiking means bugs, so again, I don't recall going a lot. I'd be willing to go on one."

"With me?"

I looked at Liam, admiring his handsome face and muscled body. "Yes. As long as we're not talking about a high adventure multi-day trip."

He turned his stick, getting the last white spot of his marshmallow over the coals. "I have the perfect place that takes about an hour to hike to. But the views are worth it."

Oh no. What have I agreed to? "By views, does that indicate a steep incline?" I practiced yoga, not scrambling up mountains. I was more of a lazy house cat than a goat.

"I promise you'll be fine."

I took my now puffed marshmallow and set it on my layers of graham cracker and chocolate then used the second graham cracker to slide my mallow off the stick. "When Meg gets back and I'm not working every waking moment, I'm game."

He smiled that delicious smile of his. The one that curled my toes. "Can't wait." I bit into my dessert, moaning in delight. Sometimes a simple treat really was the best. "It's been a while. This is so good."

Liam busied himself getting his s'more ready before he took a bite. "So true. This really hit the spot."

I stared at the dying flame as I chewed. Liam had planned a fabulous second first date. Everything about tonight gave me hope we had a future. I took my last bite and swallowed the delicious treat. "Thank you. That was really good." I held up my sticky, gooey hands. "Is there a bathroom nearby?"

Liam went to the crate by his chair. "I have wipes." He opened the container and passed me a cloth to cleanse my sticky fingers.

"All done."

Liam's eyes caught on my lips and stayed there. "What?" Did I have melted chocolate all over me? S'mores were quite messy.

Liam stepped closer to me until only a foot separated us. He lifted his thumb to my mouth, keeping his eyes locked on my face. "You have some chocolate and marshmallow stuck there." He swiped his finger across the bottom corner of my lip.

It was as though leaves dancing in the wind had got caught in my stomach and the heat from the fire followed in their path. When Liam brought his thumb to his mouth and licked the sticky substance off, my hormones went wild. Not caring if I still had goo on my face, I put a hand behind Liam's neck and pulled him toward me. I placed a hard kiss against his soft lips, letting my desire consume me. Liam's hand slid around my waist. That trail of fire followed his touch. Liam moved his lips against mine and all I could think was how much I had missed this. But if I were truly going to give Liam a second chance, it couldn't be based on physical affection alone. I had to learn to trust him again.

I broke off the kiss, burying my face in his chest. We stood hugging for a moment before Liam asked, "Is everything okay?"

I leaned back so I could see his face but still stay in his arms. "Yes."

"Good."

A few minutes later, Liam cleaned up the supplies and put out the fire. We took everything back to his Jeep, then strolled through the preserve hand-in-hand. Before I knew it, the sky had turned a deep royal-blue, and a smattering of stars had appeared. When the chilled air and mosquitos came out in hoards, Liam drove me back to my house.

My fingers twisted in my lap the whole way. Did Liam enjoy tonight? Did he want to be exclusive? Was he ready to be rid of me? I was willing to give us a second chance. Was he on the same page?

We stood on my porch where I positioned Liam's back to face the living room, blocking his view of me from anyone peeking at us from the inside. I'd learned that lesson the hard way.

"I had a great time tonight." I looked up into his glorious eyes.

"Me too."

I chewed the inside of my cheek. I wanted an answer as to where Liam stood on the matter of us, but I was also scared to find out. His actions stated he wanted a future, and I was willing to learn to trust him again. But should I let it play out naturally?

"What's going on in that beautiful mind of yours?" Liam squeezed my shoulder. "You're working your cheek so hard, you're going to bleed."

I stared at the ground. Liam had been open and honest with me today. I decided to return the favor. "Where do you see us going?" Because it felt like we'd picked up exactly where we were three months ago.

His lips turned up on one side in a cocky, teasing way. "Like on our next date?"

If I had an object in my hand, I'd throw it at him. "Yes, Liam. On our next date, because you know I'll never plan something for us to do." I rolled my eyes. "I meant our future."

He laughed. "If you want to have a DTR, just say it. Don't prance around the subject."

I did want him to define what our relationship meant to him. Or at least, where he hoped it would go. "Well, I want to make sure we're on the same page."

"What page would you like us to be on?"

"I asked you first," I challenged.

He put his other hand on my shoulder, giving me his full attention. "As I mentioned before, I never stopped liking you. My feelings have grown since I saw you at Spencer's. I'd love to continue to date one another and see where it leads us. Although. . ." He tapped his chin. "I don't enjoy the idea of you seeing other people."

My heart rate picked up speed like a boat exiting the safety of the harbor. "In other words, you're ready to be boyfriend and girlfriend?"

He met my gaze, keeping his steady. "I am."

I hadn't thought we'd get to this point so soon. At least I didn't believe I had the ability to want to let Liam back in. But I also knew Liam was special on our first date. I wouldn't have suffered if my feelings weren't so deep. At the beach, I promised I would seize this second chance. And I was the one who needled this confession from him.

I tilted my head. "You're right. The thought of another woman touching your lips stirs up violent tendencies in me. I think it's wise for both of us to give *us* our all."

His face lit up. "Excellent."

"Agreed." I grinned back.

Liam dropped his hands from my shoulders. "Thank you for giving us another chance, *Girlfriend*."

"Mmm," I hummed. "I like that title."

His arm wrapped around my waist, tugging me toward him. His finger traced along my jawline. Shivers exploded across my neck. "I do too."

Rising on tip-toes, I closed the distance between our lips, capturing his with mine. This time, I didn't plan on holding back. I had months of longing built up. I released it as I crashed my mouth against his. I slid my arms around his back, feeling the tight muscles around his shoulder blades.

The ache of missing him burned away as heat blazed a path from my chest to my lower abdomen. My heart pounded wildly. His strong hands flexed around my hips.

Liam backed me up against the vinyl-siding as he intensified our kiss. He tasted like the s'mores we had for dessert. I let out a soft moan as his mouth danced with mine. I made the right call to give him a second chance. No one had kissed me like this before and I was a thousand percent certain no one ever would again. Liam was mine, and I was his. We continued to explore one another, getting reacquainted. I had nowhere in the world I'd rather be than right here, being kissed by this marvelous man. All the while, my insides heated and sparked to life.

After my mouth was thoroughly explored, Liam leaned his head away from me.

I whimpered.

He placed one more soft kiss on my lips before taking a full step away. His lips were swollen, his pupils large.

Sign me up for another round of that, please!

"I've missed you," Liam breathed. "But if I don't walk away right now, I won't be able to stop."

"One more for the road?" I begged with puppy-dog eyes.

"Come here, you temptress," he growled.

I grinned as he pulled me into his arms once more, kissing me as if this would be our last. I didn't mind, even when the shouts of glee came from the other side of the door.

Sadly, Liam cared. He pulled back, kissing me one last time with such tenderness, I almost cried at how sweet it was. "Good night, Avery."

"Night, Mr. Knight." I slyly grinned at my pun.

Ten

My roommates pounced on me the second I shut the front door.

"How was it?" Amy asked, bouncing on her heels.

"Did you not see that kiss?" Anna's eyes were as wide as the Mississippi River. "From the looks of it, they're back together."

I pinched both their sides.

"Ouch," they yelped and jumped away from me.

"What was that for?" Anna demanded.

I pointed to the door behind me. "For staring at me and Liam on the porch. Haven't you heard of privacy?"

Anna folded her arms across her chest. "We wanted to make sure we didn't need to beat Liam up."

I rolled my eyes. "Even if it ended badly, I don't need you to fight my battles for me."

Anna's brows raised in disbelief. I got it. They saw the mess I turned into after the last time. I didn't blame them for watching out for me. I just hoped this time around we had a different ending than before.

Amy led me to the couch. "Tell us about the date."

I sat in my spot, putting my feet up on the wood coffee table. "You saw how it ended. What else do you want to know?"

"You two kissed a reeeaaally long time." Amy grinned.

I threw a blue pin-striped cushion at her. "Why'd you watch so long?" She dodged the pillow easily with her arm.

My roommates chuckled. "I could feel the heat you two were sparking. If we lived in a forest, you'd have started a fire," Anna said.

My cheeks heated as I remembered Liam's lips on mine. The way he took charge of the kiss, backing me up against the wall. The way his fists clenched around my hips. Even the sweet, close-lipped kiss he gifted me before leaving for the night. I might not make it until Friday night when we planned to see each other again.

"It was. . ." I grinned like the love-sick girl I was. "I'm going to sound so cheesy saying this, but it was knee-buckling, mind-blowing, passionate goodness."

"I'm right then," Anna challenged. "You and Liam are back together?"

I nodded once. "We are."

Amy looked at me. "Was it his kiss?" She wiggled her brows suggestively.

I chuckled. "No, not just that." I fiddled with the edge of a navy throw blanket draped over the arm of the couch. "He told me what happened the last three months. He was open, unlike any other man I've met. We can talk about anything, and everything and on the rare occasions it's quiet, it's comfortable. Also, it's like he sees me for me. He's complimentary, and I can feel his sincerity like it's visceral. And yeah, his kisses are potent."

Amy reverently said, "I'm really happy for you."

I smiled. "Thanks. I am too." I stood. "Speaking of happiness, I'm going to head to bed since I need to be up so early. I'm going to surprise Liam with dessert tomorrow after work. Friday is too far away."

"Don't you think you're coming on a little strong?" Anna asked.

Amy looked at Anna then at me, and then tilted her head toward Anna. "She has a point. You just went out."

Possibly. But I got the feeling Liam wouldn't mind if I came bearing gifts so soon after our date. "He'll tell me if I am. Besides, when we're all together for game night, I won't be able to kiss him whenever I want. I'm storing up for the drought."

Avery rolled her eyes. "Get out of here, you love-drunk woman."

"Gladly."

In record-breaking speed, I dashed home to change out of my work clothes before heading to my *boyfriend's* house. (I said it twenty times today, and it never got old.) I pulled in alongside a red car in the driveway of his townhome. Did Liam get another car? Did I misremember his house? I searched our old text thread and found I indeed had come to the correct address.

Grabbing the pink bakery box filled with two brownies, two eclairs, and two chocolate chip cookies, I made my way to Liam's front door.

Anna's words echoed in my mind. What if he didn't want me here? What if this surprise reeked of desperation? I stopped halfway from my Accord to his porch.

What was I thinking? Oh right. That I wanted Liam's mouth on mine. And just like the sugar addict I was, I'd found my new substance. This couldn't be healthy, could it?

Stop second guessing everything.

I found my courage buried deep under the riverbed of doubts and strode to Liam's black door and rang the bell. While waiting for him to answer, I spun the opposite direction, staring at the school across the street. A mother stood behind her toddler, pushing her in a swing. The child's giggle of delight carried on the breeze. A sharp pang of want hit me in the chest. One day, I wanted that. To have children. Would it be with Liam? Would a mini Avery and Liam be in my future?

The noise of the door opening caused me to spin rapidly. I almost dropped the box of baked goods, but caught it just in time to come face to face with a woman. A drop-dead, auburn-haired goddess. I stumbled back a step. "Oh. Uh, is Liam Knight here?" I again second guessed if I arrived at the wrong place. It felt a little too Dorothy-esque. I was not in Lampton, Connecticut anymore; I had landed in a nightmare.

She pouted. "No, he's not. He just started a huge new project at work and will be late. Is that a delivery for him?" She reached out to take the box from me.

Who was she? Another woman he was dating? Was he playing me? I had a hard time picturing Liam cheating on me, but it had happened before with my ex. Was I too naive and missed all the signs? This was why I shouldn't have said yes so quickly to dating Liam again. He was just like my aunt and uncle after all. I bit the inside of my cheek to stop the tears trying to form as I stood there confused and unsure. "Yeah." I shoved the box into her hands. "Thanks." I bolted to my car, fishing my keys out of my purse as I went.

"Wait," the Goddess hollered. "Who are these from?"

I flung my car door open and responded as I got in. "Liam will know." I sped off as if a tornado were approaching and I had to find shelter. My insides were all twisted up. Why would Liam ask to be my girlfriend if he was dating someone else? My heart shattered. Why would the universe put us together only to rip us apart again?

With tears in my eyes, I pulled over to the side of the road. I rested my head against the steering wheel, letting the pain course through me. Sobs racked my body. My cheeks were completely wet. What was wrong with me that I missed all the signs of a cheating scumbag? I had to give it to Liam: he had me completely fooled.

Needing peace only provided by my favorite place, I drove to the beach. Once there, I grabbed the blanket I kept in my trunk and wound my way close to the shore-line. I plopped down in the sand, watching the rhythmic waves, waiting for them to work their calming magic on my sore heart. Except peace never came. I could only think about the night before when Liam held me on the beach. He ruined my heart and my favorite place on earth. The jerk.

Eleven

The last five days were absolute chaos. Meg had posted on the Frostings social media accounts that she made it to California for *Baking Spirits Bright,* and the masses descended.

Drew and I worked from three in the morning until six at night. Each day, we increased the amount of goods we baked, and we still barely had enough. A constant headache became my companion on day three of our new vigorous schedule. By day four, my feet continuously ached. And today? I was a straight up Zombie.

Which was so not the look I wanted Liam to see at our game night tonight. I wanted to show him what he would forever be missing out on by dressing to the nines. I hadn't confronted him yet about the woman at his house because I hadn't had the time or mental bandwidth to have that conversation while I dealt with work. We'd only texted or had brief phone calls since our date. But tonight was the night to have that awful talk and kick him out of my life for good.

The door to the kitchen banged as Drew came in from the front. "Someone's asking for you," he sang.

He shoved the door enthusiastically every time he came back here, and every time I jumped like a frightened mouse.

Drew, with his blond-hair, blue-eyes, and dimples was a flirt with a capital F. I shot him down when he first got hired and ever since he only showed me his snarky side. I enjoyed the banter and didn't mind his attitude. It reminded me of my younger brother. "Let me guess." I put my hands on my hips. "A customer is mad about something and you were too babyish to handle it?"

He rolled his eyes. "Please. I'm better at talking to customers than you are. I don't need your interference."

"Then who is it?" No one knew me. Meg often posted reels of her at the bakery but never of me or Drew.

"If I knew, I would have stated *his* name when I came back to get you," he retorted.

Him? My heart thumped hard in my chest. Liam? I narrowed my eyes. "Remind me why we keep you around?"

He smoldered.

Yeah, not doing anything for me.

I snapped my fingers. "I remember now. The garbage needs to be taken out and there's a pile of dishes ready to be washed. Get to it."

"You're not the boss of me."

I gave him a condescending look. "Oh, but I am. At least until Meg comes back." With that, I sauntered out to the counter, dreading that Liam had come to see me. We needed to talk but not at my work where there were so many people around. I paused at the door separating the two rooms and inhaled a deep breath.

The second I saw him, my knees gave out. I lurched forward, catching myself on the stool we kept behind the counter. Drew ran into me from behind. Of course, he hadn't done as I asked. Our temp, Lily, shot me a worried look. I waved her off, signaling that she keep helping the customers in line before my gaze found Liam's.

His brown eyes were muddied, worry pinching the corners. "Are you okay?"

"Mmhmm." I moved the stool to my side. "Totally fine," I squeaked out through the pain throbbing in my thighs where they banged into the metal stool.

He pointed to the line of people waiting to be helped. "I came at a bad time."

I stuffed my hands in my back pockets and stared at the linoleum floor. "Told you we've been super busy."

The tips of his shoes entered my line of sight. "Avery."

I looked up at him. "Yeah."

"Are we okay? I know work's been hard this week, but we haven't talked much."

Uh, yeah, a woman opened your door, and it freaked me out. I didn't want to hear you're seeing someone or *someones* behind my back so I ran and hid like a chicken instead of facing my problem. Not an attractive trait of mine, but one that showed itself all too often when Liam was involved. I scratched my temple. "With Meg gone, I'm working all the time. I barely get to eat and sleep."

"Do you want to postpone our game night tonight? I admit, I was really looking forward to it, but if you need to rest, I'll understand."

Amy and Anna had already bought a ton of snacks, made bean and artichoke dip, and had asked that I provide brownies. Despite who Liam may or may not be seeing behind my back, I owed this group date to my roommates. I'd break up with Liam when the night was over. Tonight was for Anna, Spencer, Amy, and Lucas. "No. I'll be okay."

A customer swept by him and I automatically reached out to pull him closer to me. A huge mistake. We stood a mere foot apart. His sun-warmed laundry scent hit me. I loved that smell. Maybe even more than when the kitchen was filled with chocolate, sweet vanilla, and buttery bread baking. I took a step back.

"Okay, then." He reached out, placing a hand on my elbow. "Anything I can bring?"

I blinked. "No."

He frowned. "Are you sure you're alright?"

No, I wasn't. But this was not the place to discuss his other girlfriend. "We'll talk tonight. I need to get back to work." *Chicken.*

He frowned before placing a quick kiss on the top of my head. "I look forward to it."

I did not.

I was late getting home from work and barely managed a quick shower before Liam showed up at the exact same time as Spencer for our game night. My goal to dress up in order to break Liam's heart died on impact. Guess my wet messy bun that looked like a drowned rat matched how my heart felt. Seemed fitting.

My friends and their significant others took over the conversation from the moment the men arrived, which I was totally okay with since tonight would be the last time I ever saw Liam. There was no need for me to engage more than what was strictly necessary. Liam kept shooting me worried glances and asking if I was okay. I'd shrug and just say I was tired, which was mostly true. I was physically, mentally, and emotionally tired from work and the games Liam played with my heart.

An hour into our first game, a severe migraine hit me. Halo-spots danced in my vision, and I grew nauseous. The only thing to do was take meds and sleep in a dark, quiet room. But what about Liam? We really needed to talk.

"Liam?" I stood, gesturing for him to follow me. If I could get this over with now, I'd be able to sleep soon.

He pushed his chair back from the table. "What's wrong?"

"We need to—" A strong wave of pain rippled through me like someone was squishing and pounding my brain at the same time. I held my head in both hands, wincing through the nausea.

Liam's and Amy's voices were soft. "Avery, what do you need?" Amy asked at the same time Liam said, "How can I help?"

"Pain meds and sleep." I kept my eyes closed against the bright lights in the kitchen.

"I'll bring in some water," Anna volunteered.

"Come on," Amy said to me, leading me toward my bedroom with a hand on my back.

"Can I get you anything?" Liam asked.

I moaned. "No." There was no way we could have our talk now. Liam and Amy helped me climb into bed.

"I'll go grab some medicine. Be right back," Amy said.

Liam sat next to me, his fingers rubbing up and down my arm. "I'm worried about you. You're working too much."

"I'm fine."

"Would you like your hair tie removed?" he whispered.

"Yes, please," I croaked. It was probably a good idea, although I was not sure how someone so sweet could be so cruel.

His fingers worked swiftly, removing my scrunchie. The released pressure helped my tightened scalp. When my hair was loose, he ran his hands across the top of my head, massaging as he went. *Oh, that feels good.*

"You need to sit up so you can take these," Amy said.

Liam slid his hand under my back, guiding me into a sitting position. I cracked one eye open so I could grab the pills Amy held out to me. Anna stood behind Amy with a proffered glass of water. I swallowed and handed the cup back to Anna.

"Get feeling better, Avs," Anna said before leaving my room.

Liam gently laid me back down and readjusted my blankets.

"I'm sorry I ruined everyone's plans," I apologized to Amy and Liam.

"You haven't," Amy patted my hand, "but I am worried about how many hours you're working."

"I told her the same thing," Liam said.

I rolled over in bed, laying on my left side, hunching into the fetal position. "Meg will be back soon enough."

"If you say so. We'll let you get some sleep," Amy said with a last hand pat.

Liam's warm lips pressed a soft kiss on my temple. "Get feeling better, Sweetheart. I'll call you tomorrow." The bed bounced slightly when he stood.

I really had meant to talk to Liam. I don't know how his conscience let him take care of me when he had another woman waiting for him at home.

Twelve

♥

I sang along to "This Is Me" while I dumped cups full of flour into the industrial-sized mixer at the bakery. Frostings opened at seven, and we had exactly two hours left to prepare for the masses. Thankfully, Drew had earbuds in and left me in peace.

My cell buzzed in my back pocket, startling me. I wiped my hands on my apron and whipped my phone out. Liam's name flashed across the screen along with the photo we'd taken at the beach on our second first date. I slid my finger across the phone. "Liam?"

"Hey. I'm out front. Open up."

I glanced at the door separating the kitchen from the front counter. The circle window wasn't big enough to allow me to see anything out front, especially in the dark. "At my house?"

"No. Frostings."

I jerked my head. What was he doing here? "Um. Why? It's ridiculously early."

"Will you just let me in, please?"

Drew, in a show of unusual worry, mouthed, "You okay?"

"On my way." I nodded to Drew then walked out front, flipping the lights on as I went. Liam, in black athletic pants and a zip-up hoodie, stood on the other side of the door holding a cup holder with three to-go cups.

I flipped the lock then pushed the door open. "What are you doing here and so early on a Saturday?"

He dropped a kiss on my head before walking past me and placing the drinks on the counter. "How are you feeling?"

I stared at him. "Better than last night. Are you going to answer my question?"

He placed his hands on my shoulders, ducking to make eye contact with me. "We didn't get to talk much last night, and I figured the best way to see you was to come help. It sounded like you needed an extra set of hands anyway."

His gesture was so sweet. A theme with Liam. Time to rip the band-aid and get this over with. "Liam, we need to talk."

His brows furrowed. "That doesn't sound good."

I fiddled with my apron strings tied at my waist while fighting back tears. "Who is the red head that stays at your house?"

"What red head?"

Puh-lease. Denying she existed was such a scumbag move. I refused to look at him, still focusing on my apron. "When I dropped off the box of treats earlier this week, she answered and said you would be home late. She looked pretty comfortable from what I could tell."

He placed his hand over mine, stopping my fingers. "Avery, please look at me."

I did as he asked. I hated the way I loved his eyes when the person behind them wasn't worthy of me.

"That was my cousin, Olivia, on my dad's side. She was in town for a work conference and I offered my place for her to crash."

His cousin? I thought back to our interaction. She never said how she knew Liam. She only seemed upset that he wasn't going to be home. Was he speaking the truth?

"Really, your cousin?"

"Yep." He took his phone out and pulled up his social media account that listed her as a family member. "My cousin." He then went to his photos and showed pictures with his sister, Olivia, and him at what appeared to be a family reunion.

"Oh." I bobbed my head uncontrollably. She did not look like a cousin. But I had only seen her for a moment before immediately jumping to horrible conclusions, allowing myself to believe Liam was just like my aunt and uncle. Liam had confessed to worrying about losing me over his family drama and cutting ties first as a way to protect himself. Maybe I, too, had self-sabotaged our relationship out of fear. It was time to let that fear go. Anna and Amy had told me multiple times not everyone cheated. My own parents had a great marriage. Why couldn't I use their example as a guide instead of my aunt and uncle's?

Liam took my hand. "I promise you, Avery, you are the only woman in my life."

"I'm so sorry," I cried out. Tears rolled down my cheeks. I'd totally misjudged him. I didn't trust him and that had to change. *I* had to change if our second chance was going to work. Why didn't I believe in myself or Liam more?

"I thought you were cheating on me," I continued. "I didn't understand how you could be so sweet while two-timing me. My aunt and uncle have a horrible marriage and I've always been scared I'd pick the wrong guy. I jumped to the worst case scenario to save myself from being hurt again. I'm sorry. I will work on trusting you and asking you directly whenever I'm insecure instead of giving into my fears."

Liam pulled me into him, wrapping his arm around me. "I would never cheat on you. I'm not that kind of guy. I'm a little hurt you would ever think that."

"I know you wouldn't," I whimpered. "That's what makes this so frustrating. Why can't I let myself be happy?"

"It's hard to let go of old fears, anxiety, and past hurts in order to trust someone enough to take care of your heart. I messed up earlier. You made a mistake this time. We're going to do and say things that unintentionally hurt one another. It's life. What will make our relationship strong is being open and honest. We have to learn to trust and forgive each other. I'm all in, Avery. Are you?"

A thousand percent, yes. My heart flooded with heat as I answered with the truth. "Yes, Liam. I'm all in."

"Good." He kissed the top of my head. "Now, put me to work."

I pulled out of his embrace. "Do you even know how to bake?"

He grinned. "I can cook, and I know how to follow directions."

Those skills were better than nothing. "Can you cut brownies?"

"I don't know, that's big ask," he teased.

I grabbed his hand in mine, tugging him to the kitchen. "Come on, let's get your hands washed and find you an apron." With Drew around our conversation would be limited. But having Liam, *My Liam*, here ready to help me, I knew exactly how much he cared for me.

Liam swiped the drinks he brought and carried them with him to the back.

"Drew," I hollered.

He startled, sending me a confused look before taking an earbud out. I pointed to Liam. "This is Liam Knight. He's going to help us this morning."

Drew eyed Liam. "Have you worked at a bakery before?"

"Nope." Liam passed over a cup. "I brought drinks though."

Drew took the cup, sipped it, nodded once, and then told Liam, "Welcome aboard." He put his headphones back in and completely ignored us.

Alright then. Nice to know where Drew stood on welcoming new people into our kitchen. "I brought you hot chocolate." Liam handed a cup to me. Of course, he knew I preferred that to coffee or tea.

"Thank you." I wrapped greedy hands around the paper cup and took a small sip. Silky smooth chocolate, like drinking a melted gourmet candy bar, slid down my throat. "Mmm. Is this Belgian hot chocolate?"

He grinned. "Only the best for My Avery."

"Thank you." I got Liam situated with a few tasks while I went back to mixing the cupcake batter. I kept accidentally bumping into him, not used to having an extra person in the kitchen. The fourth time my back-side hit Liam, he snaked an arm around my waist, trapping me to his side, and whispered in my ear. "If you wanted to touch me so bad, all you had to do was ask."

Goosebumps formed on my arms, sending a shiver through me.

"Cold?" Liam whispered again, his breath teasing my neck once more.

Drew cleared his throat, staring at daggers at me. "No canoodling in the kitchen."

My cheeks erupted in flames. I did not care for Drew to get a front-row seat to Liam's flirting.

Liam smirked. "Canoodling?"

"You heard me." Drew stood his ground. "Hands off or I'll kick you out."

A laugh burst out of me, which I quickly covered with a cough. Liam stood a good four-inches taller than Drew and had at least twenty pounds of muscle compared to Drew's lean frame.

"First off," I cut-in on the stare down happening between the two men, "as the acting boss, you're not kicking anyone out." I scolded Drew. "Second"—I turned to Liam and spoke in a kinder tone—"There's no touching allowed. Meg's rule since her ex—actually, it doesn't matter why the rules are in place. We need to follow them."

Liam immediately let me go. "I respect that, Boss." He winked.

My lips tried to smile, but I tucked them in between my teeth instead. "Thank you."

The rest of the morning went by fast. Liam picked up baking quite easily. Having an extra set of hands to help box up customers' orders allowed me to clean the kitchen and start baking round two earlier than usual.

When my lunch break rolled around, I thought for sure Liam would ditch out. He'd stayed way longer than I expected. I updated Drew on where I left things in the kitchen and went out front to snag Liam for a quick bite to eat.

He was deeply engaged in conversation with a woman debating the merits of a brownie, oatmeal chocolate chip cookie, and eclair. From the way the woman fluttered her lashes and touched her long-hair, she was lapping up his attention.

Hands off, lady, he's *mine*. I strode over to Liam. "Liam?" I tapped his shoulder.

His shoulders jolted. "Oh, hey. Are you joining me out here for a change?" His eyes sparkled at the prospect.

"No. Actually, it's lunchtime. Want to join me?"

He lifted his apron above his head. "Gladly. I'm starving."

"The cafe across the street has really yummy sandwiches. Does that sound good? If not, we can go somewhere else. I just need to be back as soon as possible to give the other two a break."

"I'll follow wherever you lead."

I hung my apron by the back door, and then snatched my purse from Meg's office before guiding Liam across the street. We stayed quiet until we ordered. Liam pulled my chair out for me before sitting across from me.

"Thank you for your help today," I said. "I didn't expect you to stay so long, especially since we haven't really had time to be together. Or even talk."

He reached a hand across the table, signaling he wanted me to place mine in his. "It's more interaction than we've had all week. And I can see why you've been so exhausted."

I placed my fingers in his. "You can go home if you want."

"Not a chance."

My brows furrowed. "For real? You want to stay longer? I'm not even paying you."

He squeezed my palm. "There's no place I'd rather be than where you are."

My chest warmed like when I drank the hot chocolate he brought me earlier today. "I was trying to prove I could do it all on my own. Thank you for saving me from myself."

"Anytime." He smiled. "How about when Meg's back we take a day and go on that hike?"

"As long as we spend the rest of the night lounging around. I've never been so tired in my life."

"Yes. I'll even rub your feet."

How had I ever thought this man would cheat on me?

A waiter dropped off our sandwiches. Famished, I picked mine up and devoured half of it before I noticed Liam staring at me with an amused expression.

"What?" I looked at my shirt and lap to see if I'd dripped mustard down my front. Seeing nothing, I stared at Liam. "Why are you looking at me like that?"

"I'm admiring how you don't hold back in front of me."

I picked up the second-half of my sandwich. "What do you mean?"

"You're not afraid to be who you are around me, and I appreciate that. I don't want a fake, half, or walled-up girlfriend. I want to experience every side of you. And this,"—he waved at my face—"is exactly what makes me like you so much."

"That I'm stuffing my face?"

He laughed. "Yep."

I dropped my sandwich back in the basket it came in. "Well, if we're continuing our honesty, there's another story I'd like to share with you about why I did what I did with Olivia. And before I start, I just want to apologize again for misjudging you."

"Okay." He took a bite of his sandwich.

"In high school, I had a crush on this guy for so long. I finally worked up the courage to ask him to the girls' choice dance. To my complete and utter shock, he said yes. We had a lot of fun that night and eventually started dating."

My hand fisted. I'd vaguely told Liam about my exes, but not this story. "He was so sweet and said all the right things. I fell so hard for him. I found out two months into our relationship that he'd been seeing another girl from a different high school at the same time as me. Even though I knew you were nothing like him, I still always wonder *what-if*, you know? The same thing happened to me in college. My radar is off when it comes to judging snakes, and I really didn't want you to be the same."

He tapped the back of my hand with a finger. "Thank you for explaining that to me. Do you trust me enough now to know I'd never do that?"

I quickly wiped my fingers on a napkin before taking hold of Liam's. "With my whole heart. You're amazing, Liam. I'm so happy you're in my life."

"Good. Like I said, I'm nothing like your exes. When I'm in, I'm all in. *You* are it for me."

I swiped at a piece of hair that fell out of my ponytail. "So, all the women flirting with you today didn't spark any interest on your side?"

He held eye contact with me. "Not a single one."

I brought his hand up to my lips and a kiss on his knuckles. "I'm glad you're mine."

He smiled with soft eyes and glowing cheeks. "Me too. But we better eat and get back to work."

My brows raised. "You're seriously staying?"

"Are you kidding me? I've had so much fun today. I'm there as long as you are."

My jaw dropped. "Until six o'clock tonight?"

"My girlfriend is working. What else am I supposed to do?"

"Literally, anything you wanted."

His grin turned calculating. "And what if that's kissing you?"

Heat blazed a path from my head to my toes. "Then I'd better hurry and eat."

Thirteen

♥

F rostings was closed on Sundays and I'd never needed a break so badly. I slept in until eleven, at which time Liam magically appeared as if he had some sort of alarm that triggered when my eyes opened.

His gorgeous curly brown locks were wet, and he bent to give me a kiss in the hallway. I turned my head to the side, dodging all advances.

"What?" he complained.

I held up a hand. "I need five minutes."

I spun on my heel back to my bedroom. I grabbed the first bra I found (yay, my old nasty one), hastily buckled it, and beelined it to the bathroom where I spent an extra minute flossing and brushing. Dental hygiene was *super* important when one was swapping germs with her boyfriend.

I threw my fluffy air-dried hair up in bun before stepping out in the hallway again. Liam remained where I first saw him. "Now I'm ready for you to be close to me." I threw my arms around his neck, placing a firm kiss on his lips. My tummy swooped when he returned the kiss. "Good morning," I mumbled against his mouth.

"Morning. How did you sleep?"

I answered between kisses. "Good." Oooohhh, his lips were soft. "You?"

"Fine," he mumbled against my lips.

I chuckled, my lips still pressed to his. Liam laughed, pulling away from me.

"Hey," I complained.

"Sorry." He rubbed his bottom lip. "It tickled."

I grinned. "Yeah?" I cupped my hands around his face. His short beard scratched my palms. Holding him in place, I went in for another round. I placed a gentle kiss first before laughing again.

He knocked my hands away and trapped me in a bear hug. "You ready for brunch?"

"Is that why you came?" I spoke into his shoulder where my face was smooshed. Not that I minded.

"It is. And after that, I have a few ideas unless you want to do something else."

"This." I nuzzled my face into his cotton shirt, breathing in his fresh scent. My heart was happier and lighter after our talk yesterday. I knew from the moment I met Liam he was different. I still kicked myself for not trusting him, but we were in a good place and work yesterday proved as much. "But I do have to do some laundry and vacuum the house today."

"Okay. We can come back here. Are Amy and Anna around?"

I shook my head. "No. They're out with Spencer and Lucas."

"Even better."

My stomach let out a huge gurgle. "It is. But food?"

"Yes. We need to keep your energy up."

"For laundry and vacuuming?" I pulled back to search his eyes. "That doesn't require a whole lot."

"But we're also shopping for football food. There's a game on this afternoon, and I'm pretty sure we both have a date with the couch, or as Drew would say, 'canoodling.'"

I grinned. "I'm not sure what canoodling involves, but if it's cuddling and kissing then sign. Me. Up."

He laughed, throwing his head back. "That's exactly what it means."

Well, then. Looks like my Sunday just got even better.

"Not to sound like a broken record, but what are you doing here?" I asked Liam when he showed up at Frostings on Monday at five in the morning with hot chocolate in tow.

"Helping."

I scratched my forehead. "What about that big job you just started for your new client? I thought I wouldn't see you until the weekend."

"I can do both." He grabbed an apron, sliding it on over his jeans and gray t-shirt.

"Liam," I chided with hands on my hips. "You need to sleep. I can handle the bakery."

Completely ignoring me, he fist bumped Drew. When did that happen? I thought they disliked each other. I pointed between them with a bewildered expression before shaking my head. Whatever. They could be friends. It didn't bother me. What did was Liam showing up when he had a huge project at work he should be focusing on. He'd told me all about it last night and I couldn't wait to hear how his client liked his ideas.

"Liam, I'm serious." I grabbed onto his elbow, halting him from picking up the pizza cutter and cutting into the full-sized sheet of brownies I finished frosting half an hour ago. "Meg will be back at the end of this week and things will slow down again. You don't have to do this."

"Avery," he said in the exact tone I'd used. "I'm a grown man who can make his own decisions."

I glared at him. "And that's risking your career to help with mine?"

He set the cutter down and faced me. "I'm not risking anything. I can do both for a week. Besides, if the only way I get to see you is coming here for a few hours before work, then I will."

If it wasn't too soon to say I love you, I would. Because that's exactly how I felt toward this man who completely and utterly captured my heart and soul.

"I don't deserve you, Mr. Knight."

"You do."

I tried to be the hero that kept the bakery afloat on my own while Meg was filming *Baking Spirits Bright*. And while I knew I could have done it, I loved that I had a knight willing to swoop in and help, one who wanted to spend time with me by sacrificing his own sleep. Who taught me how to let go of my past fears and pain and, instead, learn to trust and love.

I found a good one.

Epilogue

♥

Fourteen months later

I'd barely opened our front door when Amy pounced like a Labrador.

"There's mail for you," she said as a greeting while I stomped my boots on the rug to get the snow off.

"Probably junk like most days."

She grinned, waving me inside. "Come on."

She was way too excited about my bills. My brows furrowed. "Can I at least drop my shopping bags in my room and possibly go to the bathroom before I see what has you so excited?"

"Yes, but hurry."

Sheesh, couldn't a gal get comfortable (aka remove my bra) before being pestered? I wasn't expecting anything to be delivered. The only mail I received besides bills was from a company very concerned that my car warranty had expired.

To irk Amy, I took an extra-long time changing into yoga pants and using the restroom. Five o'clock was the perfect time to tweeze my brows and push my cuticles back. A pounding on the door startled me. I jabbed my skin. "Ouch," I hissed. "Hold your horses. I'll be out in a minute."

"You need to come now. You're running out of time."

"Is there a bomb attached to it with a timer about to go off?"

"Avery, stop being a smart aleck and get out here."

I thought I heard a foot stomp, but Amy wasn't one to get overly loud so it was hard to tell. Either way, I got the reaction I wanted from her. I swung the door open with a Cheshire grin on my face. "Lead the way, ma'am."

She rolled her eyes, tugging me down the hall toward the kitchen. On the corner of the counter lay a red envelope with "Avery" scrawled in thick, black ink. I picked it up, examining every inch. This wasn't mailed; it had been dropped off.

"Who's it from?" I asked.

"JUST OPEN IT!"

"Alright, calm down." I bit my bottom lip to stop smiling. I slid my finger under the flap. Pulling out a plain white card, I again took my time to look it over, cool as a cucumber. Amy about ripped it from hands.

I opened it to a dramatic sigh from Amy and read:

To the Love of My Life,

My body warmed like an overheated oven. I didn't need to glance at the signature to know it was from my all-time favorite, hot cocoa-eyed boyfriend.

I have a surprise for you. Change out of your yoga pants and meet me at the tree farm on Main Street.

Forever yours,

Liam

My chest floated away like a hot-air balloon. The fact that Liam told me to change said how well he knew me. Instead of pestering Amy with a million questions like why she had let me waste so much time, I rushed to my bedroom. Changing into jeans and a green sweater, I took one minute to reapply lip gloss and fluff my curls before heading to my car.

Being the first week of December, the parking lot was packed. I ended up a block away at a bank. I slid my fingers into my gloves before exiting my car. The temperatures had dropped considerably the last month.

As I walked, I took in the sights of the season along Main Street. Wreaths sporting red bows decorated the lampposts. White lights were wound around the trees lining the sidewalk. Cinnamon and sugar roasted nuts greeted me as I made my way to the Christmas tree lot.

I loved this time of year. The focus on giving. Drinking my weight in hot chocolate. Eating ALL the treats. Spending time with family. Creating memories with Liam.

I increased my pace, eager to see the next surprise he'd lined up for me. He'd gone above and beyond, showering me with gifts and un-planned outings the past year. Of course, I couldn't let it be one-sided. If there was one thing I never wanted Liam to doubt, it was how much I loved him.

At the wooden stand by the chain-link entrance stood Liam in his navy coat and gray beanie. My heart thumped an erratic rhythm as I approached him. If he wore a brown paper sack, I'd still think he was the most attractive man I'd ever met, inside and out.

"Hey, Hot Stuff. I got your note."

Liam fought a smile, all while shaking his head in embarrassment. He didn't love when I called him that in public. When we were kissing, he seemed all for it.

"Will there ever be a time I'm upgraded to a different nickname? Even "handsome" would be better."

I pretended to think about it. "Nope."

His laugh rumbled against my cheek as he pulled me in for a hug. "Fine." He moved me back, putting his hand into my gloved one. "I need a Christmas tree and someone to help me decorate it. Are you game?"

"You didn't have to go through the effort of writing me a note. I would have helped you anyway."

"It sets the tone for the evening."

I looked up at him. "And what tone is that?"

His eyes had a twinkle to them, as if he were keeping a secret. "You'll see."

We spent the next hour discussing (arguing) until we finally agreed on the perfect tree for Liam's townhouse. With help from an employ-ee, we secured the fir to Liam's Jeep.

"I'll meet you at your house," I told Liam.

"Nope, I'll bring you back later for your car. Come on." He opened the passenger door for me. I climbed in. After Liam started the car, my favorite Christmas album blared through the speakers. I sang along—totally off-key—while we drove to Liam's.

We successfully got the tree in place by his large front window without any fighting. Once the tree was in the stand, Liam said we deserved a dinner and dessert break before decorating began. I followed Liam into his modern kitchen.

"What'd you make me?" I teased, hopping onto a stool at the island.

"Sorry, I didn't have time to cook. I picked up Mediterranean food earlier."

"That was very kind of you. Thank you, My Love."

He threw his hands out in exasperation. "Why can't you use *that* nickname instead of 'Hot Stuff'?"

I grinned. "I like to keep my options open. Besides, I need every other female in the vicinity to know you're mine."

"Saying *My Love* would also do it."

"Yeah, but it's not as fun." I winked.

He leaned over to kiss me on top of my head. "Ach. It's a good thing I love you, woman."

"You're not going to say *my* woman? I like it when you do."

"I think I'll stick to My Avery. Or Beautiful. Or simply my girlfriend." At that, he gave me a funny look before pulling the takeout containers from the fridge.

He'd acted like something was on his mind all night. Was the holiday season bringing up the struggles within his family? Was it something at work? I knew he'd tell me when he was ready, so I let it go.

Liam, I discovered early on, was a great cook. It was a skill his grandma taught him when he lived with her. Many of our dates were spent at home. I had zero complaints, as it often led to cuddling with heavy doses of kissing, aka *canoodling*.

"My mom called," Liam announced out of nowhere.

I dropped the fork he'd given me. "What did she want?"

"To come visit us."

Us? "Okay. When?"

"Between Christmas and New Year's."

I'd have to run it by Meg, but I could probably take some time off while she was here. Our schedule slowed down once Christmas Eve orders were picked up. "It'll be nice to meet her. What about your dad and cousins?"

"Dad's coming. My extended family is still not speaking to me."

I walked around the island and wrapped my arms around Liam's neck then placed a soft kiss on his lips. "It's their loss. You're an amazing man."

He absently nodded. His family was a sore topic and one I tried not to poke at too much.

After we ate, Liam turned Christmas music and his fireplace on. He made hot chocolate for us to sip while we decorated the tree. This moment felt like every *Hallmark* movie I'd watched. I wasn't mad about it either. It really was as romantic as they made it out to be.

With my favorite person, favorite music, favorite holiday, and favorite drink on hand, it lived up to every magical moment I dreamed about. #Reallifewasbetter.

With most of the tree covered in silver and blue ornaments, Liam pulled out a small white box—about the size a cupcake would fit in.

"Would you like to open the last ornament?"

I eyed him with curiosity, my brows scrunching together. "Is this part of the surprise?"

"It is."

I gently untied the red ribbon wrapped around the box. When I lifted the lid, I gasped. A clear glass ornament with a picture of us from when we went camping over the summer nested inside. I slipped a finger through the loop, pulling it out of the box, and watched it dangle in front of me. On the back, Liam had written, "Our first year."

Did this mean he meant for us to have many Christmases together in the future? Tears pricked my eyes. Warmth seeped from the most precious gift I held in my hand, up my arm, and into my heart, expanding it with all the love I possessed for the man in front of me.

"I love it," I whispered.

"Every year my family creates an ornament like this to hang on our tree. We pick our favorite memory, print a picture, and write the date. It's like a memory book for our lives. I thought we could continue the tradition."

I bobbed my head uncontrollably. "Absolutely, yes. Do you have any from your childhood?"

He shook his head. "Not here."

"One day will you take me to your parent's house so I can see them?"

"Yes."

I wrapped my arms around Liam's waist, breathing in his fresh scent. "Where would you like to hang it?"

I shot him a surprised expression. "Front and center. Where else?"

He laughed. "You're right. That's the best place. Go ahead."

I moved to the tree, rearranging a few bulbs before delicately hanging our ornament where I could easily see it anytime I wanted. When I turned back around, Liam was on his knee, holding out a small black box with a gold diamond ring inside.

Both hands flew to my mouth, covering my jaw that hung loose.

"Since the moment I saw your picture on Kismet, I knew I had to meet you." Liam's eyes were shiny with unshed tears. His voice wobbled. "Your humor, goodness, ability to forgive, and kindness have captured my heart. I love you, My Avery. Will you do me the honor of becoming my wife?"

My heart pounded in my throat, up to my ears, and to the top of my scalp. Heat cascaded down me as if I stood under a volcano.

"Yes!" I shouted with joy, leaping into Liam's arms. He had the foresight to close the ring box before my exuberant limbs wrapped themselves around him, tackling him to the floor. His lips met mine, with a promise of happiness.

Our mouths moved fervently together as our love flowed between us. I looked forward to many more moments like this. Liam intensified the kiss. I shifted so we both were sitting up.

Liam tugged me on his lap. My arms moved around his neck, pulling him closer. Fire, just like the one blazing across the room, consumed me. My lower stomach tightened with tingles dancing along like embers in the wind.

Liam was my everything. I couldn't wait to be his wife. I couldn't wait for him to become my husband, to be mine forever.

Best. Proposal. Ever. "I love you, Liam Knight," I whispered against his mouth.

"I love you too."

THANK YOU!

Thank you for reading my debut novella! I hope this book made you laugh at least once and swoon often. If you enjoyed it, would you mind leaving a review on Amazon, Goodreads, or Bookbub?

I love to chat with readers and gush about our favorite reads and life. Connect with me on Facebook or Instagram @authoramandapjones or even better, join my newsletter!And if you want a FREE book with another Kismet matched couple, download Jake & Isla's story here or on my website at amandapjones.com/books.

I am eternally grateful to all the amazing readers in the world. I couldn't do what I do without you, so again, thank you!

Acknowledgments

To my amazing editor, Megan—thank you for taking my vision and making it even better. Also for your compliments, especially on the kissing scene. Those are my favorite to write and I'm glad I received a fire emoji in response. My job is done. Just kidding. I have a lot to learn, but I am one hundred percent confident that heaven guided me to you. Thank you, thank you!!

To Allison Mathews for being a fabulous friend and making my writing and grammar better!

To my critique group, beta, and ARC readers. You are amazing! I appreciate all the time, feedback, and love you've shown for Liam and Avery. This book wouldn't be where it is today without you. To Melissa and Jessica for doing one last read through. You two have supported me from the beginning and I'm so grateful to have you in my corner!

I suck at grand gestures, so a big shout out to Laura Rollins, who helped me with this one, as well as all your advice on publishing. Thank you Mindy Strunk, Kasey Stockton, and Dana Taylor for answering my millions of questions while getting ready to put my first book in the hands of readers. I'm blowing you all dozens of kisses—muah!

To my husband and children. Oh man, I've worked so hard to make this dream of mine come true and you have helped me through it all. Thank you for encouraging me, understanding when I'm stressed, and eating easy dinners for months on end. Your enthusiasm for me to publish books keeps me going on the rough days. I love you!

To my Father in Heaven who has guided me throughout my entire writing career. Thank you for blessing me with the ability to bring my stories to life and to share them with others.

Also By

♥

CHRISTMAS IN CONNECTICUT SERIES

JACK & FROST BAKE-OFF Order now!

HOLLY VS. MR. IVY Pre-Order now!

KISMET SERIES

MY UNEXPECTED MATCH
FREE when you join my newsletter!

About the Author

When not reading or writing (which is rare), Amanda loves to travel, camp, spend time with family and friends, and eat chocolate chip cookies—or any other excuse she can come up with to avoid doing housework. She lives in the Rocky Mountains with her husband and three children.

44065447R00054